MW01422232

Praise for Jayne Rylon & Mari Carr's *Hope Springs*

"Be prepared for love, loss, lust, and licentiousness from beginning to end! The Compass Brothers never disappoint and neither do their daughters!"

~ *Guilty Pleasures Book Reviews*

"Once again, the talented writing duo of Mari Carr and Jane Rylon have created a beautiful love story that this happy reader could not put down. I love this series, and enjoyed every minute of this story."

~ *Long and Short Reviews*

"Any book by Ms. Carr or Ms. Rylon is automatically on my TBR list, but put them together and you have magic. *Hope Springs* is just further proof of that. [...] I guarantee you will not be disappointed."

~ *Sizzling Hot Book Reviews*

"This book packs a punch on many levels."

~ *Book Obsessed Chicks*

Look for these titles by *Jayne Rylon*

Now Available:

Nice and Naughty
Where There's Smoke

Men In Blue
Night is Darkest
Razor's Edge
Mistress's Master
Spread Your Wings

Powertools
Kate's Crew
Morgan's Surprise
Kayla's Gifts
Devon's Pair
Nailed to the Wall
Hammer It Home

Hot Rods
King Cobra
Mustang Sally
Super Nova
Rebel on the Run
Swinger Style

Compass Brothers
(Written with Mari Carr)
Northern Exposure
Southern Comfort
Eastern Ambitions
Western Ties

Compass Girls
(Written with Mari Carr)
Winter's Thaw
Hope Springs
Summer Fling
Falling Softly

Play Doctor
Dream Machine
Healing Touch

Print Anthologies
Three's Company
Love's Compass
Powertools
Two to Tango
Love Under Construction
Hot Rods

Look for these titles by

Mari Carr

Now Available:

Because of You
Because You Love Me
Because It's True

Black & White
Erotic Research
Tequila Truth
Rough Cut
Happy Hour
Power Play
Slam Dunk

Second Chances
Fix You
Full Moon
Status Update
The Back-Up Plan

Compass Brothers
(Written with Jayne Rylon)
Northern Exposure
Southern Comfort
Eastern Ambitions
Western Ties

Compass Girls
(Written with Jayne Rylon)
Winter's Thaw
Hope Springs
Summer Fling
Falling Softly

Print Collections
Learning Curves
Dangerous Curves
Love's Compass
Wicked Curves
Just Because
Wine & Moonlight

Hope Springs

Jayne Rylon & Mari Carr

Julie,
Happy reading!
Jayne Rylon

SAMHAIN
PUBLISHING

Samhain Publishing, Ltd.
11821 Mason Montgomery Road, 4B
Cincinnati, OH 45249
www.samhainpublishing.com

Hope Springs
Copyright © 2013 by Jayne Rylon & Mari Carr
Print ISBN: 978-1-61921-954-0
Digital ISBN: 978-1-61921-371-5

Editing by Amy Sherwood
Cover by Valerie Tibbs

This book is a work of fiction. The names, characters, places, and incidents are products of the writer's imagination or have been used fictitiously and are not to be construed as real. Any resemblance to persons, living or dead, actual events, locale or organizations is entirely coincidental.

All Rights Are Reserved. No part of this book may be used or reproduced in any manner whatsoever without written permission, except in the case of brief quotations embodied in critical articles and reviews.

First Samhain Publishing, Ltd. electronic publication: August 2013
First Samhain Publishing, Ltd. print publication: August 2014

Dedication

For our cousins—our first and forever friends.

Prologue

Hope Compton peeked from behind a mostly closed door into the ballroom of the local community center, which her family had rented for her sweet-sixteen party. When plotting with her cousins about how to best celebrate the milestone, it had seemed like a great idea to act grown up, wear a fancy dress and command the center of attention for once. Like the woman she wished to be someday instead of the wallflower she usually was.

The prospective fun and glamour had filled her with anticipation. Right up until she realized precisely how packed the place was. Brimming with cowboys.

Intimidating.

Her fingernails dug into the wood of the doorframe before she caught herself. She didn't want to mess up the first manicure she'd ever gotten. Her aunts had taken her, along with her three cousins—Jade, Sterling and Sienna—to the salon to help them commemorate the occasion in style. After all, they'd each turn sixteen within a year.

The opalescent, sheer polish seemed to have survived intact. *Whew.*

Despite the fact that everyone in attendance was either a relative, friend or lifelong neighbor, she wished the other Compass Girls—as the old-timers in town liked to call them—

would hurry. Surely somebody could convince Jade to come out of the bathroom without changing into her damn jeans. Bribing the tomboy with the next pick at the movies, including the dumb ones with more explosions than talking, should do the trick.

With Hope's might-as-well-be-sisters by her side, she could handle her official introduction to the crowd mingling around the appetizers they'd all slaved over. The kid in her wished she'd filched a chicken finger, or maybe one of those mini hot dogs wrapped in croissant dough, before slathering on Sterling's lip gloss.

"Quit tugging that curl." Her grandmother, Vivi, *tsked* as she approached. At odds with the chastisement, the older woman's hug generated a cocoon of safety and warmth that instantly set Hope at ease. "Your aunt Leah spent ages getting your hair just so. You look even more pretty than usual, girly. Your Grandpa JD would have had a heart attack at the thought of unleashing you four young ladies on Compton Pass. It's a blessing he only ever had boys to contend with."

"I'm not sure my fathers are going to do much better. Daddy already threatened to kick Dad out if he causes a scene." Hope smiled as she recalled the near scuffle her gown—glittery pink and off-the-shoulder, with tiers of ruffles in the full skirt—had incited. Short, it left her legs bare. Well, except for her new rhinestone cowboy boots. She adored the gift from her mom. All three of her parents had signed their names on the card, though she knew who'd picked them out.

"Silas is gonna have a rocky few years." Vivi chuckled. "Thank God he's got Colby and your mom to hold him back when boys start knocking down the door of the foreman's cabin."

"What if nobody's interested, Vivi?" Hope glanced away.

"Silly girl, what are you worrying about now?" Her grandmother didn't dismiss her out of hand. She was always there to listen when any of her children, or grandchildren, needed an ear.

"I'm not bold like Sterling, or flashy like Jade, or everybody's best friend like Sienna." Hope sighed. "I'm boring."

"Nonsense." Vivi smoothed the wrinkles Hope's fisted hands had made in the skirt of her dress. "You're perfect as you are. Straightforward, smart, observant and sensible."

"Thanks." A smile tipped her lips. She admired all of those traits, even if other kids her age might not.

"Besides, I thought you were concentrating on your future. On becoming a pharmacist. There's a heck of a lot of school and hard work between you and that goal. So when did you become boy crazy?" Her grandmother's stare dug beneath the fluffy trappings she wore today.

"You know I'm not." She waved her lovely nails in front of her. "That's more Sterling's thing. I just wonder sometimes why I haven't really ever gotten all excited about anyone. You know, like Sterling and Jade. They're always talking about Billy Hill, looking up his videos online, saying how cute he is, and arguing over which of them gets to marry him, but... Eh. He's nothing special, really. I bet he's not even fun to talk to after being so popular, so young. With everyone screaming his name during concerts and stuff... He's probably stuck up and annoying."

A musical peal of laughter rang from Vivi. "I bet you're right, girly."

"But what if I never find someone I want to get to know better?" She toyed with the hem of her dress. "All the boys in my class are dumb. They only care about fart jokes and who can punch the hardest."

"Ah, is that the real problem?" Her grandmother squeezed Hope's fingers. "Don't rush yourself. You don't have to fret about this. I agree, young men leave a lot to be desired. They'll grow up. See what they're missing. Decide they want to impress you with more than bodily functions or bravado. One day, someone will manage it too. When it happens, it happens. There's no trying about it. No running either. I knew the moment I laid eyes on JD at a dance not so different from this one—except the barn was a lot less spiffy than this hall—that he was mine. He was my counterpart. Somewhere down the road, you'll meet your other half. It could be tonight. Or years from now. Who knows? But there won't be a sliver of doubt left in that big brain of yours when you find the right person. I promise."

Vivi's ironclad belief calmed Hope's momentary panic. Why hadn't she realized the unease bubbling inside her meant she'd been worrying about this so much lately? Ever since Sienna and Josh had seemed to get a little more serious than study buddies or even friends, it'd crossed her mind from time to time. A week ago, she'd even dreamed about going to their wedding. Minus a plus-one.

Her concerns melted beneath Vivi's patient regard.

A grumble and several cheers echoed from the other end of the space as her cousins and aunts tumbled from the restroom with Jade in tow. Tomboy or not, she looked beautiful.

"Wow, Jade." Hope trotted to her cousin and held her at arm's length. "Thank you, thank you, thank you."

"You owe me a double batch of those brown sugar cookies you like to bake." Her gruff tone didn't match the smirk she wore or the glint of excitement in her striking eyes.

"All right. We've kept the guests waiting long enough. Here we go, Compass Girls." Vivi whistled, commanding their attention. The Mothers headed out to the main room to join their husbands. People clapped at the arrival of the four gorgeous women who'd made such a big impact on their community, each in their own way.

Hope beamed at her mom, who tucked in between Dad and Daddy. She did so much for people as a nurse. Through her work, she'd introduced Hope to her future career. On the weekends, Hope would accompany her mom to pick up supplies for her patients. She'd watched the Compton Pass Pharmacy owner dispense pills, check dosages and fight with doctors when he'd disagreed with the ridiculous demands of an insurance company. The ins and outs of the business had bored her cousins when they'd joined her, but Hope had been enthralled.

Like that, she'd known what she was meant to do.

Vivi promised her the same would be true when it came to picking her soul mate.

Lighthearted, she nodded to her cousins then pranced through the doorway into the main room of the community center. She linked arms with Sterling and Sienna. Jade tagged onto the chain too. They traveled as a unit toward the front of the room and the microphone there.

Her mom and dads cheered along with the rest of her aunts and uncles. Aunt Jody flicked at a tear, though she probably wished no one noticed.

As Hope scanned the room, her throat went a little dry.

"You've got this." Sterling slapped her on the flank as if she were a green horse or a recalcitrant cow. "Go ahead, welcome everyone. Don't forget to thank them for all those presents."

Hope's eyes widened as she spied the mountain of gifts wrapped in bright paper with shiny ribbons. For her. *Wow.*

"Thank you all for coming. I'm so happy you could make it here tonight. I'd like to share my appreciation for my family and all they've done to make this the best birthday ever." She couldn't remember what she'd said after that, but when she stepped away, the nod and thumbs-up from Vivi guaranteed she'd kept her composure and done the Compton clan proud.

With that, music began. People flooded the dance floor. Lots of things had supposedly changed around here since the times Vivi dubbed the good 'ole days. But Compton Pass never refused a good party.

Jade and Sterling grabbed a couple boys, whom Hope recognized as their neighbors in chemistry class. Josh claimed Sienna. Trent, whose dad worked for Hope's dads, wandered close to her. Shy and a little gangly after this past winter of growing like a weed, his voice cracked when he asked, "Wouldya like to dance?"

"Um. Sure." She didn't quite know where to put her hands, so she peeked at Sterling and mimicked her cousin's hold, though she gripped Trent's shoulders a little less tightly.

A few slow dances passed with different partners while she suffered under the glare of her Dad, who held hands with her Daddy and Mom. The experience proved to be entertaining, though pretty awkward. Her classmates didn't have much to say. Mostly, they swayed from foot to foot in one place until their turn was up. It wasn't until Dustin snuck behind her while Owen and she finished their ballad, trapping her between them, that tingles raced along her spine in a decadent shiver.

Hope trembled in Dustin's loose hold. He smiled at her and asked if she'd like to borrow his jacket.

"Thanks, but I'll be okay." Hope blinked. She glanced over her shoulder at her parents in time to see her Dad gesture to Uncle Seth, who manned the virtual music box that plucked songs off the playlists of the attendees' phones. The way he cranked his fist in a circle seemed to imply that he wanted his younger brother to broadcast something faster. The tempo of the music changed to match her suddenly racing heart, which beat at least as loud as the over-enhanced bass notes. "I think we're going to speed things up anyway. Next time?"

"Sure." He nodded.

And before she knew what had happened, poor Dustin had been swept aside by her three cousins, who mobbed her. The four of them bopped around in a giant cloud of taffeta, tulle and sparkles to Billy Hill's latest teen anthem. Why not? She'd only turn sixteen once.

They laughed the evening away.

Hope had never been as happy as when she closed her eyes and blew out the candles on the enormous strawberry-filled cake Vivi had baked. One wish in particular sprang to mind.

Late that night, as she lay wide-awake in bed, her face damn near splitting with an effusive grin, she recalled the excitement that had raced through her veins when Dustin and Owen had flanked her. Fierce and glorious, it'd left a lasting impression.

Relief unraveled so many knots inside her she feared she might melt all over her bed.

There wasn't anything wrong with her.

She'd simply failed to realize until now that she was so much like her mom.

Suddenly the need to chat overwhelmed her. Not with her parents. Some things embarrassed her too much, though she knew she could go to them with an issue if she really needed to. There was a first line of defense she would rather try. She glanced at the door, relieved to find the sliver beneath it dark. Once her parents were in their room for the night, they weren't likely to check in on her again until her dads rose at the ass crack of dawn. Ranch chores waited for no cowboy, especially not the bosses.

Hope reached over to her nightstand and grabbed her phone. She tapped the quick-launch icon on the screen. Immediately, one of the panels lit up.

"Is your bedtime later now that you're sixteen?" Always a smartass, Jade wiggled her perfectly arched brows over the visual line. Their favorite feature of their phones allowed them to keep in touch at all hours. More personal than texting, the video chats made it seem as if they shared the main house like their fathers had in their youth. Especially for Jade, the only one of them who lived off of the ranch. Her family had a house in town, because Uncle Sawyer was Compton Pass's Sheriff.

"Since when do you give a crap about the rules?" Sterling piped in as she joined their virtual pajama party.

"Ah, like you're any better, cousin." Sienna shook her finger at them all. "We have school tomorrow, remember? Don't complain when you're falling asleep during the history exam."

"Forget the past. Live for today." Sterling tipped her head. "So what's up, Hope? Get a blister from all that dancing in those fancy new boots?"

"No. I wondered..." She swallowed hard. "How the heck does a girl find *two* boyfriends?"

"Whoa." Jade sat up straighter in her black pajamas. "Seriously?"

"Yeah." She nibbled on her lower lip. "I think I'm like my mom. I want what she has with my dads. But they don't talk much about how they got together, you know? Is it weird to ask them?"

"Vivi will tell us." Jade nodded, serious for once. "We can ask her after school tomorrow."

"I've heard *my* dad talk about how stubborn *your* dad is. He says your mom and daddy had to convince Uncle Silas to join them." Sienna spoke quietly. She wasn't trying to offend. Just to inform. "He was gone for a long time. All our dads were, right?"

"Yes." Hope knew her mom and daddy had been married before her dad came home from Alaska. "So maybe I need to start with one guy and then we'll find another one together?"

Sienna tried to offer a serious suggestion. "Or maybe you should ask out the State twins. Roy and Dan are pretty funny. I bet they'd be up for a double date sans one girl."

"Those class clowns?" Sterling objected. "They're more likely to get in a spitball fight than swap spit with Hope. Or anyone else for that matter."

They couldn't help themselves. A riot of giggles and a few very unladylike snorts ricocheted between them.

"Girls!" Uncle Sam's shout echoed through the walls of his and Aunt Cindi's cottage, clear across the airwaves between Sterling and the rest of them. Heck, Hope figured she probably could have heard him bellow with her bare ears if her window had been open on the quiet spring evening. "Put those phones away or I'll tell Vivi you've been abusing your privileges again."

Their grandmother wouldn't care much. After all, she'd bought them the gadgets for Christmas. She'd stifled every single one of their parents' objections and said the Compass Girls should be as close as the Compass Brothers had been. She wouldn't stand for it any other way.

"I mean it," Uncle Sam roared.

"Okay, okay." Sterling rolled her eyes. "We'll talk more about it tomorrow."

"Goodnight," they all said in unison before clicking off, still smiling.

For now, Hope decided not to worry about dating. It seemed like a lot of drama, if Jennie Allen and her constant break-ups and make-ups were any indication. Aspirations for her career and the steps necessary to achieve them came first. Studying hard and doing well enough in school to get into a pharmacy program had to be top priorities. Someday the rest would follow.

It was enough to know what she wanted eventually. Vivi's advice from earlier in the night floated back to her. *Somewhere down the road, you'll meet your other half.* Now she knew her grandmother had been pretty much right. She fully intended to stumble across her other two-thirds.

Hope snuggled into her daisy-dotted pillow and dreamed of two strong cowboys whisking her onto one of their white horses before galloping together into the sunset.

Chapter One

Almost seven years later

"You're going to let your girlfriend throw out perverted shit like that?" John's new colleague from his residency at the hospital, Damon, proved yet again that Hope had been right to consider the jerk an unsavory influence on her boyfriend.

The asshole had enhanced too many of John's bad habits in addition to John's ever-present tendency to wallow in negativity. When she'd called him out on the changes in his personality, he'd told her she could stand to be more supportive of his evolution. Bullshit. This was regression.

She couldn't believe she'd tagged along to this seedy bar her dads and uncles never would have approved of her visiting, despite the fact that she was a fully grown, independent young woman. And now it was too late to flee because the chief prick, Damon, kept spouting off and riling his fraternity of surgeons-in-training. How could they be both so egotistical and so insecure as to shadow a dickhead like this?

Hope finally conceded to an obvious truth. She'd worried when Vivi's ancient advice hadn't held for her. She hadn't known right away that John was *the one* or *one of the ones* for her when she'd crashed into him in the hallway of the hospital. It'd taken him weeks to seduce her away from her rotation duties in the R&D wing for a crappy cup of cafeteria coffee. Because he wasn't meant for her. Never had been.

Why the hell hadn't she listened to her instincts?

Oh, right. Her cousins kept hounding her to date. And seeing Sienna deliriously happy every single day had started to weigh on Hope. Was she wasting too much time, praying for a couple of Mr. Rights to waltz into her life? Turning over a few stones couldn't hurt to speed things along, could it?

Well, look where envy had gotten her.

Hope tried to duck beneath Damon's arm. He dropped his shoulder and pinned her against the back wall of a balcony overlooking the dance floor of Two Lefts. No one came up here, really, unless they were desperate to use the dingy bathrooms beside the sparse high-top tables where she'd been sitting with John. Every time she tried to squirm around him, he trapped her tighter.

"What are you? Some kind of slut?" The reek of inferior hops permeated his stale breath. It was easy for her to detect the stench when Damon got right up in her face like that. "I hadn't pegged you for that kind of bitch, but we can roll with it if you are."

Hope prayed things would end a heck of a lot better than the slasher flick she previewed in her mind. She'd never liked scary things. Not like Jade. Or Sterling. Covering her eyes now probably wouldn't do much good when the threat was flesh and blood instead of green-screen and CGI.

Why hadn't she noticed the prick eavesdropping on the discussion she'd attempted to have with John after a few rare yet potent drinks had loosened her tongue and her desires?

Was there someone else lurking nearby who could help her escape?

She glanced around the midnight balcony of the dive near campus. She'd accompanied John against her better judgment when he'd pressured her to fit in with his new friends. Really, it'd been more of a demand. Never again. Her cousins had been right, damn them. He didn't deserve her trust or devotion.

Too bad her faithfulness would be wasted after tonight.

"Maybe she didn't mean it like it sounded. Right, baby?" When John implored her to recant her statement, his powder-blue eyes bugging out, she lost all respect for the guy she thought she'd known well enough to trust with her secret wishes. Heck, they'd dated for close to six months now. Maybe seeing Sienna so blissful had made her believe this frog could turn out to be a prince too.

Instead he probably would have given her warts if she'd surrendered to his mounting pressure to sleep with him. Thank God she hadn't. Sure, it seemed like forever. Something in her just hadn't been ready to compromise what she really needed. And now she knew he would never have been the person to give it to her. She supposed part of her had been aware of that all along and put the brakes on anytime they headed down that avenue.

Hope refused to lie about his lack of her fundamental requirements now that she'd finally embraced the bravery necessary to voice the truth. "Did it sound like I was telling you I found your roommate attractive and that I'd considered having a threesome with the two of you?"

Coward that he was, John flinched. His shoulders slumped. Then he sighed and scrunched his eyes closed as if she'd sealed her fate. When he reopened them, pretending to have a spine to stiffen, she knew what was coming.

Fitting in with his new med-school buddies had become a top priority. Straight A's slipped when he concerned himself with matching Damon drink for drink instead of correct answer for correct answer on their exams. Worse than that, Hope worried about who her boyfriend would kill someday because he'd missed an important lesson while hung-over or still hammered from the night before.

With glances that darted in every direction, Hope searched the loft for anyone who might come to her rescue. Nobody. And people on the floor below would never hear her scream above the pounding music.

A miraculous trapdoor she could hop into would be nice. She'd slide out of this hellhole as if it were featured in one of the vintage cartoons she'd loved watching with her cousins as kids. Hell, even now they occasionally splurged on an episode. They often spent evenings cycling through the cache of their streaming projector in the little house their dads had had built for them on Compass Ranch. Close to home, yet kind of on their own, they bunked together. Even Sienna and Daniel stayed over from time to time when it got too cold in the drafty RV they adored or when they grew too lazy to trek across the field after cuddling on the couch.

Somehow Hope didn't figure the aggression aimed at her tonight would disappear after a couple throbs of a blazing red thumb the size of Wyoming or a few circuits of a cuckoo bird swirling overhead. Yet pulsing lights, empty cocktail glasses and ungodly loud music left no coherent would-be knights within screaming range.

Except there—in the back corner—wearing a holographic cowboy hat, she thought she recognized one of the ranch hands. Boone. After all, how many of those glitzy things could there be in Compton Pass? Sure, the town had grown a bunch since the days her parents, and grandma Vivi, told tall tales about. But it still had nothing on a metropolis like New York or San Francisco. At least from what Uncle Sam and Uncle Sawyer would have her and her cousins believe. They should know based on the time they'd spent on opposite coasts.

Hope had one time put a few of the guys in their places when she'd overheard them bullying Boone. She'd let them know Compass Ranch wouldn't tolerate such ignorance. Even in these supposedly more enlightened times, it wasn't always fun to be gay in a rural town where people's mouths ran faster than their sense. She'd made those dumbasses eat their words. Over that very same hat.

Or one just like it.

Too damn bad the glam topper didn't seem to belong to an ally. She could have used Boone to return the favor right about now. Glitz bobbed down the spiral staircase in a hurry. Hope didn't blame the innocent bystander for extricating himself from the disaster about to happen.

She remembered how frightened she'd been, standing up to those jerks in the barn. But being home, on Compass Ranch, had guaranteed her safety. These pricks didn't realize the entire oncology ward of the hospital they roamed daily had been named in memory of her Grandpa JD.

"Are you even fucking listening to your man?" One of the sloshed residents leaned in so close his spittle dotted her cheek.

"Nah. I think she was too busy checking out that dude." Another one shook his head as he closed the ring tighter around her along with his cronies. No chance of escape. "She's ready to spread her legs for any guy who'll take her. Sorry, bitch, that homo's not interested in what you've got."

"But if you're that desperate, maybe we could give you what Johnny here obviously hasn't. We won't leave a pretty thing like you panting." The nastiest of the bunch sidled up to his pals. "After you've had us, you won't want anyone else."

"I'm pretty sure you're right about that." Hope's skin crawled. She drew her hands into fists at her sides, banking on bluster to propel her for a bit. The odds couldn't have been less in her favor. Still, the self-defense tactics that her dads and uncles had insisted on teaching her and her cousins—their daughters, the Compass Girls—would make these tyrants pay, just a little.

"What's the matter?" Gross Guy wiped his sweaty hand across her face, in what he must have thought was a sexy pawing. "Getting cold feet already?"

A shudder seized her at the thought of this cretin over her. Abusing her body and soul. Taking what she'd saved for someone special. How could she ever have believed John might be that man someday? In truth, he was just a scared, lonely boy.

"Too late to bite your tongue now." The other guy lowered his hand. In the gloom she couldn't say for sure, but she guessed he fondled himself as he prepared for whatever they had in mind. "You already confessed you wanted to be used by a bunch of guys."

"That isn't what I said at all." Defying them would never enlighten them. How could she explain to these animals the love she'd witnessed all her life? Sure, her mom's and dads' relationship couldn't be called conventional. That didn't make the affection they shared less real. Everlasting.

"Go ahead," Damon goaded her boyfriend, who'd wasted no time getting trashed on arrival. "Give her what she wants."

John nodded. "I've been waiting for this for *fucking* ever."

"She's been holding out for all of us." Damon corrupted the last shred of decency John possessed.

"Maybe you're right. You'll like this, won't you, Hope?" He smirked. "You said so yourself."

"No," she whispered. "Don't."

"She practically begged you to take charge." Damon instigated trouble. "Where are your balls? Be a man. Give her what she asked for."

Too bad a real man would have hauled off and broken that asshole's nose then stormed out of there with his girlfriend in tow. Hell, Hope wished she could have done it herself. Except she didn't have the chance.

John ripped the lovely retro peasant blouse Jade had given her for her birthday straight down the center. The gaping wound in the floral print displayed her breasts, which played peek-a-boo over the top of the lace-trimmed balconette bra she'd borrowed from Sterling.

How wrong they'd both been about how tonight might end up. She no longer appreciated the false advertising of the push-up cups.

Hope didn't gasp. Or cry. Instead, she got pissed. How dare they ruin so much for her?

Of her?

She gulped, feeding her agony to the flames of her rage. Her mind skipped to things she *could* control. The aftermath. Her cousins would be there for her. They'd help her recover her sanity once these savages circling her did their worst. She had to tough this out, draw on the steel Compton genes she knew she possessed. Later, she would make them pay.

Justice. She would fight for it.

Some of her bravery wavered when all her righteousness failed to distract her from the reality descending on her in ghastly slow motion. Their charge seemed to take forever. And yet it passed in the blink of an eye, before she could change the course of her future.

When Damon reached into the wreckage of her shirt to fondle her, something inside her snapped. A feral growl erupted from her throat. She yanked up her knee, taking advantage of John's mesmerized distraction to smash her joint into her *ex*-boyfriend's balls. Hard. Next she jammed the knuckle of her curled middle finger into the eye of the dirt bag who was too sloppy inebriated to react fast enough and dodge her violent outburst.

By the time she swung for the third, they'd caught on to her struggling.

It didn't take much for the remaining couple of guys to restrain her. They pinned her arms roughly behind her, putting her on display for their pals without a care for her nearly dislodged shoulders. Damon's ruddy cheeks had nothing on the heat in his unswollen eye when he rounded on her.

"You fucking cunt," he bellowed. "You're going to pay for that."

"Damon, this is getting out of hand." Doubled over, John tried too little too late to diffuse the disastrous outcome of *a few drinks with my new friends.*

"You're right. Someone should have taught this whore a lesson a long time ago."

Hope braced herself, but it didn't matter. The force of Damon's backhand whipped her head around. A supernova exploded inside her brain, brighter than the neon laser designs flickering across the dance floor below. The wail she'd planned to unleash came out as more of a sick moan.

Force ripped her from her captors.

The floor rushed up to welcome her, except it wasn't a comforting embrace she fell into but a hard, sticky surface instead. She clawed at the asshole who advanced on her prone form. When he grabbed for her leg, she kicked out, satisfied by the thump of her heel connecting with...something squishy. The wrench of her ankle felt like a medal of honor.

Except her resistance only enraged the posse. Like the wasps that had stormed from the nest she'd accidentally stepped on in third grade. A swarm of attackers clouded around her. Someone yanked her waist-length hair while another flipped her none-too-gently onto her back.

Wind gusted from her lungs at the jarring contact accompanied by the heft of two guys settling on her shoulders—one on either side of her head. Ringing in her ears kept her from hearing their insults clearly. In fact, she would have sworn one of them yelled, "What the fuck?"

Right before the whole night went insane.

Even crazier than it had already been.

The flashy hat returned.

Righteous rainbows gleamed from every facet of the garish accessory like sunlight off a white knight's sword. The beacon stabbed her abused eye. Her courage began to crack. Splinter. Help had arrived. She tried to use the cowboy's diversion to clamber to her feet. Noise and chaos didn't seem to influence the ogres mashing her to the dirty club floor, though.

At least until bodies started flying. John jetted through the air and slammed into the wall behind her with a sick crunch before landing in a crumpled pile.

"You fuckers will pay for this." A vaguely familiar man warned them, but the attackers had been too riled to retreat without a fight. Adrenaline and pack mentality drove them to see this nonsense through. "You have no idea who you've messed with."

Another guy took a hard hit from a launched fist, then crashed into the dirty bathroom door, falling through it onto the even scummier tile inside. A startled shout from a man at the urinal followed by a stream of piss on the intruder might have been funny under other circumstances.

"You think you assholes are so tough?" Damon circled Boone's comrades, a pair of broad-shouldered silhouettes.

Oh, thank God. The cowboy must have joined some ranch hands for a night on the town. He hadn't abandoned her. He'd called in reinforcements of the badass variety. And he'd come back. If nothing else, workers on Compass Ranch were loyal. Fiercely. They had more in common with family than employees.

Hope would have sobbed with relief if her face didn't hurt so damn bad.

"Hell, no. We're practically kittens compared to the Compass Brothers." That rumble had her attempting to concentrate. Shadows surrounded craggy features. Nothing could obscure the obsidian flare of the man's distinctive eyes. She stared up into the dangerous glint of Wyatt Ellison's charcoal glare. "But her father, *Silas Compton*, is the meanest son of a bitch I know when he's pissed."

"And, oh *shit*, is he gonna be pissed," portended the second man. No mistaking the pair now. Not with voices like those. Steel wire and molten glass. Sienna said Clayton Fisher could melt chocolate when he talked. And Jade swore Wyatt had a perfect, sculpted chest that would make you want to lick the sweet liquid candy off him. Her cousin claimed the scenery was a large benefit to her job on the ranch. Probably true. All of it.

Clay and Wyatt went together like grilled cheese and tomato soup.

Comforting. Delicious. Ooey-gooey goodness she wouldn't hesitate to pop into her mouth.

Hope's heart raced when she recognized her pair of saviors. Great. The two men she'd least like to witness her humiliation were the duo that had stumbled upon her, broken and disgraced.

"If you run now, we'll let you keep your head start." Clay attempted to defuse the situation one last, pointless, time.

"We're not afraid of three cocksuckers like you." Damon closed the deal. He lunged.

Wyatt took him down as if he were as weak as a newborn foal. "Have it your way."

The efficiency of his leg sweeping beneath his opponent in a burst of speed impressed Hope, distracting her from her fear and pain momentarily.

Out cold, her attacker didn't budge even when Clay gave him an extra kick to the ribs to be sure he wasn't playing possum. Hope's cowboy commando reached next for one of the men crushing her while Clay confronted the other.

Boone spared her the trauma of witnessing the two good guys soil their hands for her. He hunched over her, protecting her and assessing the damage all at once. "So sorry, Hope. Jesus. I can't believe they did this to you. Right out in the open. It went to shit so fast. Oh, damn. Damn. I ran as quick as I could. I didn't stand a chance on my own. I'm no brawler like these two. I'm so sorry, darlin'."

She would have reassured him, except just then Wyatt and Clay checked in. Their ragged breathing billowed their chests as if they were stallions who'd been put through their paces.

Wyatt shook his hand, flinging droplets of blood from his mangled knuckles.

Hurt, because of her.

"Gotta get out of here." She wanted nothing more than the security of her cozy cabin in the heart of her family's empire.

Only there would she feel safe again.

When she tried to stand, her trembling body refused to obey. A yelp bubbled from her when her torqued ankle lit up. She slipped from Boone's grip and tumbled to her hands and knees on the nasty floor. The entire gallon jug of bulk antibac she kept at her workstation in the hospital wouldn't be enough to sanitize her after this. She might have to borrow the second stash she kept at Compton Pass Pharmacy, where she worked as a tech on the weekends until someday…when she planned to make an offer on the place. Mr. Murphy had to retire soon. Something made her wonder if he delayed for her to finish school.

The trio of men above her unintentionally added to the agony zipping through her. She hated letting them see her when she was literally down. Gritting her teeth, she banished the physical agony bombarding her.

"Good news, guys, I know what painkillers to request." She tried to laugh off her injuries.

"Shush." Clay collected her into his arms and cradled her against his chest. His unbreakable hold still managed to be gentle. "Don't go thrashing around, either. Let us see where you're hurt. Hurry, before it gets crowded up here."

Already people had begun to mill around the staircase as they came to use the facilities and found them occupied with unconscious losers. The accidental golden shower administrator hustled past, attempting to flag a staff member. A bouncer or three would join them any second. Probably not a bad thing. A couple of the losers on the floor began to moan.

How had a night on the town gotten so out of hand? She licked her lip and tasted blood.

"Sweetheart, I know you're not going to like this, but we've got to call your Uncle Sawyer." Boone was the voice of reason.

She tried to object. Sadly, Wyatt and Clay agreed, outvoting her by a landslide.

"Your dads will kill us if we don't." Boone smiled at her, distracting her from the throb in her cheekbone. He tossed a look at the man holding her. The sadness in his eyes had her whimpering again. What had he been doing up here alone anyway? "You wouldn't want Clay to risk his pretty face, now would you? I'm kind of fond of it. Plus, I *love* my job. Don't get us fired, please."

"Dad would never..." She cut off with a wince. Actually, he might. When it came to her safety, not even Daddy or Mom would be able to talk the pillar of Compton Pass down.

"Exactly. So do this the right way. Report these fuckers. Then they'll never hurt another girl again, either. Please?" Clay soothed her. From his heavy visual exchange with Wyatt, he simultaneously sent the other man a message. "It's important to have the scene documented."

The most imposing cowboy took a deep breath and let it out slowly. Whatever Clay had silently told him must have worked. Wyatt leaned over and braced his palms on his knees, staring at his friend as if inspecting the other man for damages. Just as Clay and Boone had done for her.

"I'm good, Wy. It's okay. We're all all right. This is Hope Compton. Not..." He stopped at Wyatt's wince. His gentling reminded her of the way her daddy, Colby, could settle her dad, Silas. The cowboys were right. Her father would freak. He'd probably tear apart half the state looking for these creeps if she didn't put off her selfish needs for just a bit longer. If justice didn't reign supreme, he'd be tempted to administer cowboy law.

She could hang in there.

Long enough to file a complaint with the sheriff. Her uncle. "Shit."

Boone laughed. "Uh huh."

"I've never heard you curse before." Wyatt smiled. The unexpected sunshine from the too-serious man dazzled her. They hadn't spent a lot of time together, but they'd passed each other in line at ranch barbeques and had exchanged hellos when she visited Jade in the barn. Enough for him to notice her conservatism, she guessed. Wouldn't take much when compared to her cousins. Even Sienna was more fiery. "I like it. Naughty is cute on you."

How could anything look adorable on a roughed up woman? Ugh. Somehow Wyatt had seemed to understand she'd never needed to feel even a tiny bit attractive more than right now. His intuition lent his suggestion more credibility.

"Call him." She couldn't manage more around the lump in her throat. Not to mention the split and puffy lip that grew two sizes by the second.

Hope relaxed, curling into Clay's chest. She had to prepare for the whirlwind about to descend on them all so she could shield her trio of saviors. Her family could be...overbearing. The heat and protection of Clay's hold made it easy to surrender to the bone-deep exhaustion filling in behind her ebbing fear.

"That's right. You close your eyes. Lean on me and forget everything else for a bit. We've got you." He carried her to a dark leather couch across the balcony and sat with his back to the rest of the club. His broad shoulders blacked out the commotion beginning to boil nearby as word of the altercation spread.

Hope's fingers restlessly kneaded the solid pectorals beneath her hands. She didn't realize what she did until Clay's groan startled her from her trance. When she looked up, she was surprised to find them not alone. How long had her mind wandered?

Wyatt stood guard while Boone directed traffic.

A wince restarted the warm trickle of blood down her chin when Wyatt barked a demand for Sherriff Compton. The voice-activated feature of his phone responded in a hurry.

Before she could change her mind, her uncle barreled down on them all, en route to the bar.

"So you want to tell us what sparked that shitstorm before Sawyer shows up?" Clayton tried to straighten her hair. His fingers didn't tug even when they encountered a snarl. Patiently, he worked the knots loose, putting her in order.

Hope sat up a bit, trying to avoid staining his shirt until she realized bright red speckles had already marred the light blue of his soft cotton. Not to mention the ragged tear in his other shoulder. She made a mental note to replace his ruined clothes.

"John was my boyfriend." She rolled her eyes when Clay shot her an incredulous glance. "I know. Feeling pretty stupid about that. Still, not as dumb as I feel about admitting to him, here, that I intend to try a ménage someday."

Before she could blink, Wyatt appeared at her side. His hand cupped her cheek and tilted it up so she couldn't help but stare into his sympathetic face. "Not everyone understands that kind of relationship. Like your parents have. You have to be careful, Hope."

"But you do?" She looked between Wyatt and Clay. Then to Boone, who nibbled on his bottom lip. "You get it?"

"We should." Clay interjected when Wyatt sputtered. "Since the three of us *gave* it a shot. We also know it's nearly impossible to last like that. For us to find that perfect guy or girl to make us a trio that won't kill each other...well, I don't know if it'll ever happen."

Hope blinked a few times. "Really?"

Sure, her parents argued every now and then. Never about anything serious, and never for longer than it took for them to kiss and make up. But Wyatt? And Clay? *And* Boone?

Wow. She honestly had never guessed.

Boone turned away. She wondered again what he'd been doing upstairs alone if they'd come as a unit. Or were they a pair and an ex? Or maybe three exes? The permutations were more difficult for her to contemplate at the moment than calculating the therapeutic index of a particularly complex drug.

"Yeah. It isn't as easy as your parents make it look." Clay murmured to her. A sigh raised and lowered her on his shoulder. "A relationship between two people is tough enough. Add another layer and… Yeah. We've only dreamed of getting all that in harmony for long. It's a nice thought, though."

A million questions raced through her mind. She might have asked them if Wyatt hadn't rendered her speechless by tugging his black T-shirt over his head and tossing it to her. Washboard abs proved Jade right—he had the nicest body she'd ever seen on a guy. Including movie stars. Okay, well, she hadn't seen many others unless the ranch hands counted.

In her estimation that gave her enough experience to appreciate his spectacular physique. A shiver wracked her.

His pupils dilated at her reaction but he otherwise ignored it. "Here. Put that on. One of the deputies just came through the door. Sheriff Compton can't be far behind."

Clay sighed as he relinquished his hold on her just long enough to help maneuver her sore limbs through the material of Wyatt's shirt, which still radiated his warmth. It smelled amazing. Like soap and man and maybe hay. A flash of something—premonition, she supposed—granted her a glimpse of herself giggling between these two cowboys as they stargazed on a late spring night. Every fiber of her being screamed, *Yes*!

"What is it?" In tune to her reactions already, Clay peered into her eyes. The concern and affection he leveled at her did funny things to her core.

Uh oh.

She *knew*.

Chapter Two

"Hope!" Sawyer Compton charged the loft of Two Left Boots. "Hope, where are you?"

Wyatt rushed to meet the man at the top of the stairs, glad they were on the same team. Facing off against the rampaging sheriff would have been extra unpleasant. He would have done it without hesitation for the pure girl nestled in his partner's arms. "She's over here. Clay's got her."

The sheriff's face transformed before Wyatt's gaze as the seasoned law officer canvassed the room. Stony, he took in the trash littering the floor. Then his mouth pinched and a muscle in his jaw twitched as he noted the blood soaking through Clay's shirt. Finally, his countenance relaxed as he registered the three Compass ranch hands protecting his brother's daughter.

When Hope peeked from behind Clay, the early signs of a shiner in progress were clear. Sawyer cracked his knuckles.

"They didn't get much further, but I wish like hell we'd shown up a few minutes sooner." Wyatt kicked himself for the distance they'd allowed Boone to shove between them. Honestly, he'd been relieved when the other man had opted to slum for a fuck buddy instead of sticking awkwardly by their sides. Their friendship might never recover from the mistake he'd allowed them all to make. That didn't mean he didn't root for the guy to find what happiness he could. It had to be more than he'd gleaned from Wyatt and Clay.

"You did your best. Thank you," the Compass Brother rasped to Wyatt without taking his stare from his niece. "I owe you boys. Our family does."

Wyatt didn't bother to tell the guy their actions had nothing to do with Compton clout and everything to do with the ghosts of his past paired with common decency. Never would he let a woman be brutalized again if he could stop it. Clay knew. Wyatt couldn't survive failing another girl.

Like he had Kiri.

Taking his silence as acceptance, Sawyer strode around the sectional and crouched by Clayton's knee. He held his arms out to Hope and muttered in a gruff tone, "Ah, baby. What did they do to you? I'm here. No one's going to touch you again."

The gorgeous girl in Clay's arms sobbed. The dam broke and tears rained down her cheeks after dangling from her thick, curled lashes like diamonds. Shock and something like jealousy—toward Clay or Hope, he wasn't sure, maybe both—speared Wyatt when she refused the solace her uncle offered and nestled closer to Wyatt's man instead.

Whoa.

Sawyer Compton looked up, his raised brows making him appear as stunned as Wyatt.

Despite the power that radiated from the man all three cowboys in attendance respected, Clay didn't hesitate. He embraced the young lady they'd admired from afar and supported her with the quiet sureness he'd granted Wyatt in the darkest hours of the night.

He knew just how tempting it was to believe in that relentless affirmation of peace ahead. It built confidence that the world would come to rights again soon.

Unlike Wyatt, Hope didn't show her appreciation by fucking the shit out of Clay, though maybe she would have given it a try if her uncle hadn't lingered a hairsbreadth away. The clench of her swollen fingers on Clay's nape just before she buried them in his ultra-soft tawny hair gave her away.

Now this was trouble they didn't need.

Because Wyatt felt it too. Something swirled between the three of them. Endorphins could account for some of the exhilaration storming his better sense. Not all of it, he suspected. Watching Clay melt, his restraint dissolving in the wake of Hope's tears, Wyatt had to act.

He closed the gap between them and laid his hand on Clay's other shoulder. While Sawyer studied them, he squeezed, reminding the other guy of his presence and where they were. Now wasn't the time to find another stray to take in. How had that gone with Boone?

Thankfully, his partner stiffened. His caresses on Hope's spine morphed into awkward pats. The woman sniffled and blinked. Those almond eyes of hers nearly cracked both him and Clay when she darted a wide, watery stare between them.

Damn, she was potent.

"I—I'm sorry." The questions in her eyes at Clay's sudden change punched Wyatt in the gut. It had to be better to stop this before it got started, though. No sense in misleading her. Certainly not when the stakes were so damn high. They couldn't afford to lose their jobs. It would kill them to leave the place they'd come to love as if it were their own.

"You're fine." Clay tucked a strand of hair behind her ears. He likely couldn't resist. Wyatt didn't blame the guy either. "Just, maybe you'd better tell your uncle how this went down. Sooner you do, sooner you can go home."

Mention of Compass Ranch and that cute little bungalow she lived in with her wild cousins made more moisture trickle from her eyes. She bit her abused lip, then nodded.

Hope couldn't believe she'd survived the past hour. Or two, she supposed. Somehow the aftermath seemed worse than the attack itself at times. Embarrassment stained her cheeks all over again as she recalled admitting to Uncle Sawyer that she'd instigated tonight's drama by blabbing her secret wish to the wrong guy. He'd only nodded, but she knew it wouldn't be long before her mom came knocking at her door with some follow-up questions.

Ack. Mortifying. Relief mixed in with her dread, though. It might be nice to unveil her true aspirations to her mother, the one woman who could understand and offer advice.

Just not tonight, please.

She glanced at the mirror on the back of the passenger's visor in Compton Pass's ancient cop cruiser, which Uncle Sawyer called a classic. Whatever. She couldn't help the giggle that rose in her at the sight of three badass cowboys smooshed together like ducks in a row behind the metal mesh dividing the guys from her.

Wyatt's shoulders easily took up more than his fair share of the bench seat. His bare chest drew her attention and reminded her that she wore his shirt, while his tree-trunk thigh pressed to Clayton's from hip to knee where they both tried to spread their legs out. Poor Boone was squished into the minimal remaining space. He'd even had to remove his hat to fit.

Right as they turned into the gravel parking area in front of her house, a stab of pain in her cheek reminded her of the damage there. All designs of scurrying inside and tucking into bed without any more commotion were squashed when a booming call reverberated against the windows of the car.

"What the hell is this, Saw?" Her father marched up to the patrol car, peering into the rear of the vehicle as his brother climbed from the better-days Chevy. Hope averted her face, dodging the beam of the motion-activated light her Uncle Sam had installed on the Compass Girls' home. "We came to bring the girls some leftover strawberry pie from Mom. They got awful twitchy when we realized Hope wasn't here. I don't know where the hell she is. They wouldn't crack. Probably out all night with that weenie she's been dating. And now you're bringing me three dumbasses to deal with? What'd they do? 'Cause I'm not feeling very lenient at the moment. Give me a reason..."

In the rearview, she saw Clayton wincing. The ranch hands were trapped by the doors that only opened from the outside. Like fish in a barrel, they waited to be put out of their misery.

"Shit." She gritted her teeth even as Wyatt chuckled. She thought she heard him murmur, "*Still cute.*"

Then she flung open her door and stepped from the car.

"Hope Elizabeth?" Her dad's voice had *that* tone to it. The one that meant he teetered on the cusp of erupting. "What the—?"

"Hang on, Si." Always the voice of reason, her other father offered her a chance to set things straight. She took it.

"Daddy," she whispered as she stepped into the beam of brightness, which probably highlighted the damage like a stage spotlight. "It's not as bad as it looks. Okay?"

"Jesus." Colby blanched, his face seeming to glow in the shadows. For a moment, Hope thought he might get sick. Then he devoured the space between them with his long strides and ran his knuckles ever so lightly over her puffy cheek. "Little one, no. Someone hit you?"

"Don't worry, Daddy." She hugged him tight around his waist. "I punched him back. As hard as I could. Pretty sure there's at least one guy who won't be having kids anytime soon either."

He chuckled, though the strangled sound held no amusement. "That's my girl. We'll get your mom out here to take a look. She'll make sure you're okay."

Hope nearly lost it again when he rocked her in his gentle hold as if she were made of glass. She knew he wouldn't trust anyone's judgment but her mom's. And not because she was a nurse.

"Your shirt. What are you wearing that enormous baggy thing for?" Her dad, Silas, clenched and relaxed his hands repeatedly before he could keep going. "What the fuck happened to your clothes? Somebody start fucking talking. Right. Now."

Uncle Sawyer cleared his throat when her dad roared. "Maybe we'd better go inside, call Lucy. You know, settle down a minute before we dig into the details?"

It wasn't that easy to derail Silas Compton.

"Did these little bastards dare to lay their hands on you?" Her father grew so still and so quiet, Hope wrenched from her daddy's light embrace. With Colby gawking after her, she threw herself against the patrol car to keep her dad from destroying the wrong people.

"No." She stared Silas straight in the eye and defused his mounting rage. Uncle Sawyer mimicked her refusal, but her dad only looked at her. "They fought for me, Dad. Bloodied their own hands to protect me when I got myself in trouble. Don't you dare bark at them. Or worse. They deserve so much better. For sticking up for me when I was stupid."

"Hope—" Uncle Sawyer tried to calm her. No use.

Now that she was home, everything seemed too much. The nightmare of the evening, her dashed dreams, and the intensity of the reaction to the guys penned in behind her... It was more than she could handle.

She turned and pressed her unswollen hand to the glass of the window as she bent at the waist to peer inside. Clay reached over and matched the gesture. She swore the pane heated between them. Wyatt's eyes turned molten as he stared into hers, then clenched Clayton's knee.

Linked, she smiled her goodbye with a nod to Boone thrown in. Then she fled.

"Hope!" Her dad bellowed, but she didn't pause. As she stumbled up the stairs, she was glad to see her cousins and Daniel pouring from the front door. They surrounded her and drew her into their oasis, insulating her from the world outside.

At the last second, she stole a glance over her shoulder. Enough to see her father lend a hand to Wyatt as he unfolded himself from the patrol car. Uncle Sawyer did the same for Boone, then Daddy extended his arm to Clayton, clapping each man on the back as they joined their elders—bosses, mentors and idols—for what was sure to be a graphic debriefing.

God help her.

"Holy shit, Hope." Sterling hugged her as they tottered across the threshold. "When you go bad, you really do it right, don't you?"

Tears mixed with laughter as her universe tilted again, returning to somewhat normal. "Guess I'm talented like that. Can I tell you about it in the morning?"

"Go. We'll try to deflect the Mothers. I'm sure they're on their way by now." Jade waved toward the stairs to their bedrooms. "Hurry so we don't have to lie when we say you're in bed."

"I love you guys." She slumped in their group hug, pleased when Daniel ruffled her hair from his place behind Sienna.

"Compass Girls rule." Sterling slapped her ass. "Go."

Chapter Three

A knock rattled Hope's bedroom door on its hinges. Brisk yet steady, the rap made it easy for her to guess who made the intrusive noise before her grandmother poked her head through the opening she forced. "I'm old, girly. I don't have time to wait for you to quit moping."

Hope couldn't help the smile that led to a wince. The entire right side of her face felt disfigured this morning. She didn't have to consult her mirror to know it was at least as bad as she speculated when Vivi's eyes bulged.

"Well, I haven't seen one of those in a while. Used to be a staple around the house when your dads and uncles were growing up." She *tsk*ed. "Did you at least put some frozen peas on that thing?"

"Seriously?" Hope gingerly prodded the area with her fingers, measuring the swelling that inhibited her vision.

"Works like a charm." Vivi spun on her heel. Considering she didn't have to shout her request for produce, there were at least a few more visitors waiting in the hallway.

"Oh, jeez." Rehashing the night before a million times didn't hold any appeal. "Invite them in, Vivi. Let's get this over with already."

Before she'd finished granting her permission, the space flooded with concern and distraction from her various relatives.

Sterling, Jade and Sienna didn't know any boundaries. They crawled into bed beside her, still in their pajamas. Sienna leaned her shoulders against the headboard beside Hope while Sterling and Jade lounged at the foot of the mattress. Her aunts were hot on their heels.

Vivi stood beside her. She grasped Hope's chin and angled her face toward the light. "Yeah, nothing some cheap veggies can't fix."

"I'd like to be the judge of that." Hope's mother approached, squeezing in beside Vivi.

Hope tried not to let her eyes mist in the first few seconds they saw her. She'd save that for the retelling of the attack. Crap. But she couldn't deny the comfort and welcome relief her mother's touch infused. As she had last night, Lucy examined her daughter. Several quick tests later—mashing on her cheekbone, which hurt like hell but supposedly not enough to warrant an X-ray, rotating her arm in all kinds of directions, prodding at her bruised knuckles, then tending to the scrapes and cuts on her hands, knees and lip—Hope was cleared for duty.

And the rest of the slack they'd been granting her vanished.

"Tell me what happened." Her grandmother perched on the edge of the bed and took Hope's undamaged hand in hers. "I heard a version from Sawyer, but I want it direct from the source. Don't leave anything out. I have a feeling your uncle wasn't entirely truthful. So fill us in on what he wanted you to share."

"Oh, um, well..." She glanced up at her mom and squirmed a bit. "I'm guessing he didn't tell you what started the fight."

"He mentioned that you wouldn't be seeing John anymore." Vivi huffed. "I can't say I'm sad to see him go. Even if it weren't for this insanity, and what his friends did. You didn't have the sparkle, you two. He was never right for you."

"You're right." Hope groaned. "Next time, could someone mention this before I waste six months of my life on a loser?"

"What did he do?" Aunt Leah propped her hands on her hips from where she stood with Aunt Cindi and Aunt Jody. "Do we have to hurt him?"

"Pretty sure Wyatt took care of that." She winced. "He's not going to get in trouble, is he? Not Clayton or Boone either, right?"

"My dad said they're clear of all charges." Jade assured her.

"Now that..." Vivi narrowed her eyes. "*That's* what I'm talking about. Something happened between you?"

Hope cleared her throat. No use in trying to lie to women who knew her at least as well as she knew herself. "Yeah. Sort of. It was an interesting night."

"Back to the guys who beat you up." Lucy wasn't ready to let go so quickly. "Why, Hope? What did John do?"

"Actually, it was my fault." She stared at her fingers where they played with the edge of the quilt Vivi had made for her when she was little. "I had a few drinks. At the club, they poured them stronger than I'm used to. I told him—"

Sienna squeezed Hope's knee when she stalled. "Stop talking crap. This could never have been your fault. No matter what you said to your boyfriend, he didn't have the right to lay a hand on you. Or the right to let anyone else hurt you. Uncle Sawyer said there were several guys in jail last night."

Hope nodded, then continued, "I told him that someday I'd like to try a threesome and that I thought his roommate was cute." Oh. My. God. The admission nearly stuck in her throat.

"Whoa." Sterling whistled. "You hadn't even let him touch you and you were talking about another guy?"

"Well, yeah. Why lie?" She peeked up at her mom. The woman had a gentle smile on her face. Certainly no recrimination hid in her electric blue eyes.

"So he didn't take the news well and decided to hit a woman?" Aunt Jody seemed like a flight risk. Any second she might grab a shotgun out of the locker by the front door and demand to know where John lived.

"No, no." Hope didn't like the thought of being responsible for murder. John was weak and a complete jerk, but there was no sense in ruining both their lives over someone so insignificant to her future. "Not him. His friends were there. Damon."

"I told you I didn't like that guy." Jade glared at Hope. "Liam says he's a complete asshole."

Liam owned a neighboring ranch. Half the time, Hope couldn't figure out if he was Jade's best friend or her worst enemy. Jade pointed at her. "Remember the time I saw him looking up your skirt when you were climbing the stairs to your workspace in the hospital?"

"I should have listened. He overheard me talking to John. Things got out of control." She gulped.

"He tried to rape you. *That's* what Sawyer didn't say, isn't it?" Vivi very rarely lost her temper but Hope could feel her trembles, transmitted through the mattress springs.

"Him and his friends. John included." Hope ignored the tears that overflowed her eyes again. They'd go away soon enough. "I fought them as hard as I could. I wouldn't have broken loose in time. But the ranch hands stopped them."

"I'll be inviting those boys to Sunday dinner." Vivi nodded. "Maybe every week for the rest of the year."

"I won't argue." She'd love to see Wyatt and Clay again. Boone too. Maybe she could pry some answers out of him.

"Then it's settled." Her grandmother smiled. "I'll stop by the barn to talk to Jake and..."

The elderly woman blinked. As if she realized what she'd done, she stalled, waiting for one of her granddaughters to bail her out of the tricky situation. They'd gotten used to covering for Vivi in the past year. Her memory seemed to decline by the season.

"Jake is already coming." Jade stepped up to the plate this time. "I talked to him this morning. I'm sure he won't mind letting the guys out early under the circumstances. I can invite them when I head in for my chores this afternoon. Save you a trip to the barn."

"Thank you," Vivi said quietly.

In the dim space Hope couldn't be sure, but she thought she detected a glint of fear and sadness in her grandmother's eyes that had nothing to do with the violence of the night before. It broke her heart and hurt ten times worse than the impact to her face had.

All the Compass Girls exchanged glances. They knew Vivi was grateful for their support in her ruse. They'd agreed to this charade to give her some semblance of normalcy following her diagnosis of Alzheimer's disease. It wouldn't be long before they got busted. And oh would the Mothers be furious then.

Hope had wondered lately if it might be time to revisit their pact. What if Vivi forgot something at the wrong time and it put her in a bad situation? They couldn't deny the holes in her memory were getting bigger and seemed more plentiful lately.

So it surprised her when Vivi said, "I want to tell you girls a story. A long time ago, when I first started dating JD, things were wild."

The Mothers joined their daughters, everyone cramming onto the mattress with their legs crossed or tucked beneath them. Vivi's memories were precious, even more so now. The

Compass Girls had never met their grandfather, so they'd gotten to know him through the millions of anecdotes their family and all the residents of their town had shared with them. The girls had been collecting them. Recording them in a journal.

They'd add this chapter to the rest of Vivi's legacy.

"He was older than me by a bunch, you know? A lot of people in town said we'd never last. They thought he was using me." She snorted. "As if he gave a damn about my family's land."

"Anyone who knew you both could see you had him wrapped around your little finger." Cindi reached across to pat Vivi's knee. "He adored you. Nothing meant more, not even this ranch."

"Later, yes." She smiled as her eyes took on a faraway look. "Those beginning times, though. Not as much. He was so in control. Authority oozed from him naturally. I was innocent and foolish enough to know no fear around him. I think that's what attracted him, actually. Nobody talked to him like I did. He ensured I was unafraid to ask for what I wanted. JD would have given me the moon if I desired it. He kept me safe and allowed me to experiment with whatever caught my interest, a rare luxury for a woman in those days."

"Hell, maybe even now." Hope deflated as she let out a huge sigh.

"Not with the right man. Or men." Vivi reassured her so simply and easily, Hope could have bawled.

"See, JD had heard folks talking about Charles, my boyfriend, and me. He knew we were serious before he strutted into that barn dance. But when he saw something he wanted, he wasn't the kind of man to be deterred." Vivi tapped her toes to a beat only she could hear. "He told me he never wanted me to regret hooking up with someone so early, before I'd had a chance to try other men. We had an instant attraction. He was willing to talk to Charles about it. To see if...we could work something out. Charles refused. He got jealous. Angry. He wanted to own me. It didn't take me more than a moment to realize I was about to make a horrible mistake. So I broke it off. JD came to my house the same night. He promised that with him things would be different. I'd always be free. He'd make sure I had what I needed. But he refused to be my one and only man. Not until I was sure I'd signed up for eternity with the right mister."

"On one hand, I totally don't want to know. But I have to ask...you slept with other guys while you were dating Grandpa?" Sienna seemed a little horrified.

"Of course not." Their grandmother crossed her arms over her chest. "Without JD, sex meant nothing. With him, it was everything. From the most romantic to the naughtiest things we tried. Like inviting another man to play along."

"I'm not hearing this." Sienna put her hands over her ears and pretended to hum. At least for a moment, until curiosity won out.

Hope agreed. It kind of grossed her out to hear about the ancient exploits in her kinky family tree. Still, the idea that she might not be a total freak kept her from objecting in the spirit of too much info.

Some of her other cousins didn't seem to have any such reservations.

"You and Grandpa JD had a ménage?" Sterling leaned in closer. "Go Vivi!"

"We did. More than once. But unlike Lucy, Si and Colby, it wasn't a forever thing. It was fun. And temporary. While JD shaped the trysts into the perfect experiences for me, I understood pretty quickly that only he held the key to my heart. After that, it lost some of its appeal. Plus, our playmate Landon found a woman he was serious about and ended up marrying her quick, before she could get away."

"Wow." Jade looked at their grandmother with wide eyes that only got bigger when Aunt Cindi cleared her throat.

"Go ahead, Cin." Lucy waved to Sterling's mom. "Share. It could help, please."

"What?" It was fun to see Sterling shocked for once. "No way. Not *my* mom. Ack! It's so much cooler when it's someone else's parental unit."

"Oh, shush. Listen, Hope, I lived on Compass Ranch for a while before your Uncle Sam came home from New York. I never had a place of my own, really. I was insecure about family, and loneliness ate at me. For me, ménage was a way to feel grounded. A part of this place and something more important."

"Seriously, Mom?" Sterling rose up to her knees. "Does Dad know?"

At first Hope thought Sterling might actually be horrified. Then she realized Cindi had just gained a ton of admiration from her wild daughter.

"Oh, hell yeah." Aunt Jody laughed. "Your mom doesn't do anything half-assed either. She didn't settle for two guys, but a barnful from time to time. It went on for years after she hooked up with your dad. He likes to show off, that one."

"Okay, Mom, we probably don't need *all* the details." Sienna winced.

It was good to hear Vivi and the Mothers laugh, even if their amusement came at the price of their children's squeamishness. When they'd settled down, Vivi stepped in. "All I'm trying to say, Hope, is that a real man knows what his woman needs. Unconventional or not, he'll find a way to grant her wishes. If John couldn't be that man for you, forget him. Embrace the one, or ones, who fulfill your desires. The ones who understand you and make you complete. There's nothing wrong with what you asked of your boyfriend if that's what you really need right now. It was *his* damn fault this happened. His reaction is the shameful one. If I ever hear you call yourself stupid again over this, you'll have me to deal with. Understand?"

Somehow she was certain Vivi wouldn't forget that threat.

"Yes, ma'am." She relaxed for the first time since John had started shouting at her the night before.

"Good. You should know better. You've seen your mom and dads all your life. They couldn't be any other way than they are. Trust me, they tried long enough. Until they were all together, something just wasn't right." Vivi reached out to squeeze Lucy's hand. "I know you're looking for something similar, at least you told me once you were."

Hope nodded.

"It's tougher when there are lots of people to consider. Yourself included." Aunt Cindi nodded wisely.

"These boys—the ranch hands—are they the ones?" Vivi grilled her.

"I'm not sure. I hardly know them." She ignored the fairytale part of her that screamed, *Yes, you do!*

"Mmm hmm." Vivi didn't look convinced. She squinted at Hope, tapped her foot a few times, then smiled.

"I mean... I'd like to get to know them better. But who knows if that's even what they're really into? Or if I am." She sighed.

"Trust your instincts. Don't second-guess yourself, Hope. Please. Dooming yourself to traditional because you think you must be crazy...or greedy..." Her mother's raspy entreaty rent Hope's heart. "You can't force something to be everything when it's only a piece of the puzzle. I got lucky. You might not. If you think there's a possibility that Wyatt and Clayton are your guys, you go out and get them. Don't let them run. It's hard, baby."

"That's what they said last night." Hope seemed to shock them all with her admission. "They tried a poly relationship and it didn't work out. I'm not sure they're up for another shot."

"With Boone," Jade murmured. "That makes sense now. They've been acting so odd around him lately. Extra polite. Poor guy. I think I'll try to pair up with him more during our shifts."

"Things that seem impossible are sometimes the best, once you win them against outrageous odds." Aunt Jodi cracked her knuckles. They knew how she'd fought for Uncle Seth.

"Jody's right. You're strong and smart. You've done the hard part. You've opened up and admitted your heart's desire. If you backtrack now or try to take the easy way out, you'll be miserable for the rest of your life." Aunt Leah tossed in her two cents. "I don't think any of us found it a snap to land our Compass brother, but I can honestly say the effort was worth the reward."

They looked to Vivi. Long faces guaranteed they thought of her late husband. Vivi smiled. "Leah's right. I wouldn't change one minute of my years with JD."

"We made it through, and we're stronger for it." Her mom stared at her a little too shrewdly. Did she suspect the secret they were keeping? "When you go through something like that together, it's not likely you'll break apart easily. Family, friends, lovers—the bonds were tempered in the flames of that time. And they're holding."

"You girls will be the same. I know it." Vivi nodded to her grandchildren. She smiled at Sienna, who'd already claimed her forever guy. "Who could resist a Compass Girl?"

Hope yawned, the restless night and her aches catching up to her.

"Time for you to take a nap." Her mother shooed people from the bed. "I'll go get you a pain blocker and I'll have your dads bring up those peas, okay? Ignore all their blustering and let them see you're just fine. Besides, they have a lot of experience with black eyes. Have to say, though, yours is a hell of a nice one. Going to be pretty purple for a while."

"See you in a bit, Hope." Her cousins waved as they trickled out, Sienna last. "Daniel is baking those brownies you love."

"Mmm." She smiled. "Thank you. All of you."

Suddenly, their departure set her adrift.

"Vivi, wait." Hope snagged her grandmother's wrist before she could get very far. She swallowed hard as her mother nodded then filed from the room behind her aunts.

"What is it?" She put her arms around her granddaughter and held on tight.

"You were right, Vivi." Hope tried not to nibble on her abused lip.

"Usually am." She laughed. "About what this time?"

"Last night...after...when I was sitting with Clayton and Wyatt. I felt something between us." She inhaled until her tweaked shoulder objected. "*I knew.*"

This time Vivi was the one with tears in her eyes. "I'm so glad, Hope. They're nice boys. Handsome too. I swear I've seen Wyatt staring at you before. I have a good feeling, girly."

"It's crazy, though, isn't it? What if I'm wrong?" She blurted out her worries. "What if it was some adrenaline high because of what happened? What if they didn't feel it too?"

"Hush." Vivi petted her hair. "Don't get ahead of yourself. I don't doubt for a minute that your instincts are right. You've never had a false alarm before."

"John—"

"You never felt *it* for him." Vivi waved away her token protest. "Don't try to fool an old lady, huh? We won't even talk about the rest or I'll have to hunt John down. It was doomed before he revealed his cowardice."

"Maybe." She hated to admit the truth.

"Let's see how Sunday dinner goes." Her grandmother stood, dragging Hope out of bed and toward her closet with a surprisingly strong grip. "Show me your prettiest dresses. We'll have Sienna curl your hair so it drapes over your face a bit. It's... What day is it today?"

"Tuesday, Vivi." Hope tried not to wince.

"Right. So we've got five days. I bet makeup still won't be quite enough to cover the bruising. If I know decent men, they'll feel guilty for not rescuing you sooner. But you're going to knock their boots off. I can't wait to see how they look at you. *I'll* know."

"Are you sure that's a good idea?" After last night she might not be comfortable flaunting herself. What would they think of her showing off a few short days later?

"Hell yes." Vivi wagged a gnarled finger at her. "And if you dare try to say it's inappropriate I'll take you over my knee. I'm not as feeble as you think."

"Oh yeah?" Hope laughed when Vivi pinched her.

"Try me, filly. I'm not done with this rodeo just yet." Her grandmother whooped as she flung open the closet door.

Chapter Four

Three days later, Hope retrieved a deposit bag from beneath the counter of Compton Pass Pharmacy. She'd picked up extra shifts to help distract her from the drama at the hospital, where Uncle Sawyer had made sure John, Damon and the rest of the gang were no longer welcome. Everyone kept asking her why. It got tiring. All she wanted was her quaint hometown store where customers appreciated her warm, efficient service and the medicine she doled out.

Worry about the impending Sunday dinner, plus some pesky nightmares, had kept her up late almost every night. So she had to concentrate as she filled out the paperwork clipped to the bills she tucked into the maroon pouch. A half dozen people had actually used cash for their transactions today. Compton Pass really was antiquated sometimes.

A strip of leather with ancient sleigh bells stitched to it clanked against the glass door, the tinkle dulled by years of corrosion. Hope braced herself then glanced up from where she closed out the register. A sigh of relief escaped before she could stop it.

"Don't say it," her little brother, Austin, warned. Her younger cousins—Doug, Bryant and James, the Compass Boys, they liked to call themselves—filed into the retail side of the store. The pharmacist had rolled down the gate and locked up the drugs before racing off to his grandson's basketball game.

Normally being alone while closing the store didn't bother her. But Monday's disaster still had her on edge.

The Compass Boys' bikes leaned against a sign on the sidewalk outside. Though James was old enough to drive, they preferred to ride most everywhere, with horses on the ranch and those ten-speeds in town. They may have been teenagers, but she could easily imagine them growing up to be like her dad and uncles. Already they stuck together and ruled their world. "Maybe we just happened to be over this way when you were getting off."

"I can take care of myself, guys." She barely resisted dusting her fingers across the fading bruise on her cheekbone. The lie pinched a little. If it hadn't been for Wyatt, Clayton and Boone...

"Sure you can." Austin flipped the sign on the door to *Closed* just as someone appeared over his shoulder. Two cowboys, it looked like, though she couldn't detect more than their hats and loose swagger clearly through the tinting on the plate glass that protected the store from the blazing summer sun, which cut through the unpolluted Wyoming air.

Things might be less than modern in her hometown, but she found that refreshing. Unlike the smog-filled canyons she'd seen on TV.

Hope tried to wave to the would-be customers. A little inconvenience was nothing if they needed help. In the rural area, they still didn't have all-night establishments. For that matter, not much opened on the weekends either. If it was critical, they'd have to go to the emergency room or do without until Monday morning. Or after work, as most folks couldn't stop in before quitting time. She didn't want anyone to suffer needlessly.

"James, go see who that is and what they need." A tilt of her chin in the direction of the receding shadows tipped off the young man. "Hurry before they get back in their truck."

When he ducked out, she wondered if she should have sent him alone. After all, the absolute lack of contact from John had her looking over her shoulder as much as her male relatives if she were honest. Why hadn't he bothered to call? Apologize? Offer some explanation for his temporary insanity? Check on her? Anything to prove she hadn't made a colossal error in judgment for the past half year running.

James returned, panting as though he'd had to jog to catch up to the quick-moving pair. "Don't worry, it was just Wy and Clay."

This time her heart did pound triple time.

And not in fear.

"What did they need?" She chewed the inside of her lip. Damn, she should have popped out there herself. Resisting a detour past their cabin on her way home each night had been nearly impossible. She'd even found a few reasons to visit Jade in the stable. The partners hadn't been around the couple times she stopped in. What if they didn't want to see her? It wasn't her usual day to work. Maybe they hadn't expected her to be here?

"Dunno." He shrugged. "They said they wouldn't hold you up and that they were fine. Glad we were here to look after you."

All of the boys' chests puffed out at that. If the two ranch hands trusted them to protect her, they must be doing something right. Wyatt especially wasn't known for taking shit from anyone. He was one of the lead hands. He had supervisory duties along with the day-to-day stuff. Men respected him. Leads didn't last long otherwise.

Had they been checking up on her? Were they worried about retaliation from the guys at the bar? Jade swore they'd asked about Hope and her recovery first thing every morning at the barn this week. Knowing they cared even that much warmed her heart and a few other places too. Plus it made her feel better about her inquisition aimed at Jade each evening. When Sienna had mentioned that Wy and Clay had stopped by the Compass Girl cottage Tuesday afternoon, she'd nearly shrieked at her cousin for not waking her.

Unfortunately for her, all parties involved had agreed she looked like she needed the rest.

None of them had realized her insomnia had more to do with steamy dreams of the pair of cowboys retreating into the sunset without her than with fear or recovery from her thankfully minor injuries.

Were they passing each other in endless near misses on purpose? Or did they want to be chased?

She'd find out soon enough. No one turned down one of Vivi's seats at dinner. The tradition in the main ranch house was an honor, plus the food made a damn fine reward in and of itself.

Two more days.

"You okay, Hope?" Doug, the youngest of the bunch, tapped her elbow.

"Fine. Just tired." She scooped up her purse, the keys to the truck and the deposit. "You guys riding home with me? I'll need to stop by the bank on the way."

"Sure," Bryant said. He held the door while Austin and James began loading bikes in the back of her hand-me-down, extended-cab pickup. "Plus we can get some candy from Dever's next door while we're waiting."

"Better not ruin your appetite." Hope felt old when she chastised them.

"Have you seen that kid eat?" James chimed in. "I don't think that's going to be a problem."

"I wouldn't talk, asshat." Doug loved to curse. Maybe because he was the littlest. "You eat almost as much as Daniel."

Their discussion unraveled into a playful debate filled with insults and a few light punches. Everything seemed normal, yet not. Hope was glad they occupied the silence while she thought of Wyatt and Clayton and every possible reason they might have come to the store, then left without so much as a hello.

Waiting until Sunday to get the answer might prove impossible.

Saturday afternoon rolled around and Hope was still wondering about the pair of cowboys and their motives. She blinked as she realized her daydream of Clayton and Wyatt showing up on her doorstep wasn't quite as ephemeral as she'd imagined. Hell no, one of them was really here. At her house.

Even after she blinked and scrubbed her eyes, the sexy man approaching didn't disappear. Half of her fantasy climbed the porch stairs. She overlooked the whitewashed decking from her window seat, where she curled up with her e-reader and stared blankly, distracted from her favorite romance novel.

She hadn't gotten past the first chapter before she'd superimposed herself and her heroes on the characters inside. Too bad the traditional story didn't conform to her desires.

Without rushing, she took the chance to study the leaner, taller of the two cowboys who'd starred in every dirty thought she'd had since the attack nearly a week ago. And boy, had there been a lot of those. Because reality was, she'd meant what she'd said to John. About craving a ménage. Except now she knew who she wanted to have that chance with—Wyatt and Clayton, who knocked at her door with his long fingers curled into a fist that reminded her of his strength.

His affable nature only went so deep behind his soft brown eyes and the dimples at the edges of his quick, broad smile. In a once-was-white sleeveless tank partially tucked into tattered jeans, she got the feeling he'd left home suddenly. A leather cord around his neck kept an arrowhead pendant close to his heart.

Did he always wear that beneath his outer shirt? The raw materials complimented his tan skin and the earthy quality he had. Grounded, natural and easy to get along with—at least according to his peers.

Yes, she craved him. Along with his best friend. Speaking of... Where was Wyatt? They rarely ventured out solo. Or so she'd been told by the people she'd interrogated while she nosed around this past week.

His brusque raps shattered her stud-watching session and launched her from her perch. Thankful the rest of the Compass Girls had gone into town for a movie and dinner at the new BBQ joint, she dashed for the entryway. At the last possible instant, she fluffed her hair in her simple ponytail then smoothed the wrinkles from her yoga pants and T-shirt before opening the door.

"Hi, Clayton." A smile covered the nervous tremble of her lip. At least, she prayed it did. "How are you?"

"Me? *I'm* fine." He whipped his hat off and scrubbed his other hand through his too-long hair. "I'm so glad you're here..."

"What's wrong?" The heat of his hand warmed her palm, though she hadn't realized she'd reached out. All her frivolous thoughts fled as soon as she noted the worry lines creasing his forehead and the tightness at the corner of his eyes.

"I hate to ask, but I need a favor." A light squeeze on her fingers made her eager to promise the world. If only he wouldn't let go. The connection that had blazed through her when he'd scooped her to his chest *that* night still burned bright. For her at least. It hadn't been an artifact of her gratefulness. Genuine attraction tugged them together.

One worry crossed off her list.

"I'd say I owe you a good turn. Or six." The silhouettes of the brutes that had surrounded her materialized in her mind. "Tell me. How can I help you?"

Hope mentally slapped her forehead. She sounded like a girl in one of the porno recordings Daniel had snuck onto their digital projector and Sterling had refused to delete.

Still, he didn't resist when she towed him across the threshold, suddenly imagining repayment in the form of a killer blowjob. Well, okay, he'd have to teach her how to suck him. But she was a good learner. Jade had assured her no guy would turn one down and that they all would appreciate that form of repayment, sloppy or not.

Mind! Stop that!

"Hope?" His head tilted as he evaluated her flushing cheeks.

"Uh, yeah." She cleared her throat. "Sorry. What did you say?"

"It's Wyatt. He's sick." Clayton paced on the plank flooring of the informal foyer. "Do you think you could come take a look?"

"I'm not a doctor." All thoughts of seducing the young ranch hand flew from her mind. Clay wouldn't be here if it they were talking about a case of the sniffles. These guys were strong. Most of the men on the farm were. "But I've gone with my mom on her rounds forever and I took a lot of classes for my degree. What symptoms does he have?"

"Uh..." Clayton hesitated. His glance at the tracks his muddy boots left behind struck her.

"If you want me to help, you can't bullshit me." She wondered why she seemed to lose all her inhibitions around him. Her cousins would have gasped to hear her curse.

"Right." A groan fell from his mouth. Usually curled upward, the flat line of his lips seemed especially grim. "Wy's going to kill me. But he's burning up. Sweating, chills, his color is messed up. He's having weird dreams. He can't stomach food and..."

Hope ran through a plethora of potential diagnoses until he dropped in the last piece of the puzzle.

"His hand is twice its normal size. It looks like a goddamned grapefruit on the end of his arm. It's hot to the touch and a nasty shade of gray." His gorgeous eyes seemed sad when he met her gaze for the first time.

"The same hand he mangled on those jerks' faces?" She winced. As if there was any other answer.

"Yeah." Clayton clenched his jaw. "He let Doc Anderson take a peek a couple days ago. He prescribed an antibiotic, but we haven't had time to get into town before—"

"Fuck!" She clapped her hands over her gaping mouth.

"Someday that's going to be funny." Clayton winced.

"Why didn't you guys come in that day? James told you I'd reopen the register! Hell, I'd have given the medicine to you for free. You could have started a tab and caught up with Mr. Murphy later." She trembled with shame, regret and fury. *Dumbasses*!

"Wy didn't like the idea. He didn't want you to feel guilty." Clay sighed. "He's going to be pissed I'm even here, but..."

"This is nothing to mess around with. He could lose the hand if the infection spreads. Hell, it could kill him. What prescription did Doc write?" She curled her fingers around as much of Clay's wrist as she could and dragged him upstairs toward her bedroom despite his protests about his dirty shoes.

Doc served as the ranch vet, though he had originally been a physician in the messed-up world outside their slice of heaven in Wyoming. When he'd had enough, he'd moved here and changed his course, preferring to spend his time with animals instead of men, though he'd kept up on his previous trade, just in case.

Right now she could understand. Humans were cruel, and stupid. All of them. The male variety especially.

"Will he be okay?" Clayton asked softly.

Maybe this one was different.

"We'll do our best. Think, Clay. What was on the paper Doc gave Wyatt?" She jogged into the bathroom she shared with Sterling, then dug for the pills leftover from when her cousin had recently had her wisdom teeth lasered out. Another hardheaded Compton, Jade had refused to heed the warnings on the bottle and had quit taking her medicine when she'd determined it was safe instead of abiding the directions to continue the full course. Said she didn't want to risk her birth control pills malfunctioning.

Hope rolled her eyes. God save her from obstinate friends.

"I couldn't make it out," he growled. "Damn it!"

"It's all right." She clasped the amber plastic cylinder in her hand before turning toward Clay. The raw worry in his expression hit her in the gut. A few steps closed the gap between them. Wrapping her arms around his waist, she laid her cheek on his chest long enough to measure the galloping of his heart. The cool stone of his necklace pressed between them. Its chill heated rapidly. "This isn't going to be strong enough to combat an advanced infection, but it'll do to start. Let's get it to him, help him relax, get as comfortable as possible then we'll see where to go from there. Okay?"

"Thank you." Clay threw his arms around her. He crushed her to his long body, burying his nose in her hair. "You don't understand how much this means. This isn't how things go between us. Wy takes care of me. I've known him forever and I can't recall him ever being sick."

"Unless there was a lot of alcohol involved, huh?" Hope attempted to lighten the mood.

"Wy doesn't drink." Clay separated them and shifted toward the door. Intermission over. She threw alcohol, bandages, antibiotic cream and a few other goodies into a toiletry bag. They raced down the stairs and out to his truck as he filled her in. "Even before he cut himself off entirely, it was never to excess. He refuses to get out of hand—lose control."

Interesting. She filed that nugget away for later. Maybe Jade would know more about Wy's dry mandate. They bounced across the rough patches of gravel paving the ranch road as they headed toward the cabins housing pairs or trios of cowboys.

"Hope." Clayton drew her attention to his white-knuckled grip. "He's not going to approve of me bringing you to our bunkhouse. I don't give a shit. He's too weak right now to fight us. Trust me. I can hold him. If you have to, just go for it. Examine him. Do what you've gotta do. I'll cover your back."

She swallowed hard.

"He'd never hurt you, honey. Not on purpose." Clay must've caught her hesitation. "He's just not used to letting anyone see him with his guard down. He'll hate every second. Likely, he'll try to escape. When we won't let him, he'll lash out. It's his way. A show to make you run. However he can. Don't believe a word that comes out of his mouth. It's not true, though that might not make his poison hurt any less. Ignore his words, look into his eyes. You'll be able to get an honest read from them no matter what he says. Promise?"

"Yes. I understand." She regretted that her situation had caused either of them this pain in addition to the emotional discomfort she was about to inflict on Wyatt. Not to mention the melancholy in Clay. How many times had Wyatt pushed him away that he knew the drill so precisely? "But I think he'll find that people underestimate me. Never a wise move with a Compton."

"Amen." A hint of Clayton's dazzling smile returned when he measured her.

Both of them kept quiet and prepared themselves for what waited as they skidded into the worn dirt patch where the guys typically parked their truck. Clay hopped down and rounded the hood as she gathered her supplies. Before she could slither from the bench seat, his broad fingers were encircling her waist.

He lowered her to the ground gently. Both of them gasped when he rubbed her along every inch of his body. Electricity arced between them. Something to consider. Later.

Wyatt attempted to sit straighter and suppress his shivers. Finger-combing the hair stuck to his forehead in sweat-soaked clumps was impossible given the raw state of his hand. Who knew one banged-up set of knuckles could reduce a guy to this? Okay, so he hadn't exactly been able to keep the dressing clean, or even on, while working the ranch. Shoveling shit was actually part of his job description on occasion.

Another wave of blackness washed over him. *Holy shit.*

He didn't scare easy, but he'd be lying through his clenched teeth if he said he wasn't freaking out inside. Another hour or two and he'd be begging Clay to take him to the emergency room even though they both knew that if he ran into anyone from Monday night at Two Lefts, he'd start swinging again.

It must have been bad for Clay to ignore his demands and retrieve the one woman he had struggled to hide his pain from.

Hope marched toward him. Instead of the pity he feared, he saw anger. It looked sexy on her. So different from the docile woman he'd assumed she was inside as well as out. The fire she'd kept hidden did freaky things to his head.

Unless that was another side effect of the germs raging through his bloodstream.

He had to get rid of her quick, before things got out of control. She couldn't handle him, and definitely not both him *and* his best friend. Look what had almost happened to her just from discussing a fantasy. Compton Pass wouldn't be her safe haven anymore if she got tangled up with them. No way would he have that on his conscience. One innocent girl was plenty to torture him for life.

"Are you stupid?" She shook his shoulder. "Is this how you take care of yourself?"

"I'm not the one who was dating some asshole who threw you to the dogs."

She winced. Maybe because of his classless reminder of her bad choice, or maybe because of the fear shimmering in her gaze at the memory of what had nearly happened in that dump.

"Ah, fuck." He reached for her, but the bone-deep ache in his knuckles stopped him from making contact. "Didn't mean that."

"He's crankier than a stallion with his nuts in a vise." Clay glared at his partner. "Probably 'cause he's hurting so bad. Not that he's got much patience to start with."

Despite his harsh proclamation, the unusual grooves bracketing Clay's sinful mouth declared his partner's anxiety loud and clear. "I'll be fine. Just tell me you've got some medicine. Or know where to find some on the ranch."

"My mom…" Hope began to offer, her pretty smile erased when he shuddered and locked his jaw to stifle a groan.

"No. She'll tell the foremen." Wyatt shook his head with enough vehemence to make the world rock inside his feverish brain. "Can't afford not to work."

"You've earned time, haven't you?" Innocent, she obviously believed in the system.

"He has." Clay developed that stubborn set to his shoulders. The one that turned Wyatt on any other time. Even did a little now, not that he could do much about it.

"I don't call off," he snarled. "Ever."

"If you think you're going to survive the pasture in the next week or so, you're nuts." Hope bent at the waist to get right in his face. The angle gave him a nice peek at her cleavage and the top swells of her pert breasts.

"Watch me," he growled. The aggression might have been more effective if it hadn't turned to something like a whimper midway through.

"He needs intravenous antibiotics. Something way more potent than these." Hope extracted a bottle from her messenger bag.

"Please, may I have them?" Wyatt gritted out an appeal.

Both Clayton and Hope turned to stare at him.

"What're you looking at?"

"Just making sure hell hasn't frozen over." Clay blinked. "Don't think I've ever heard you say the P word."

"Yes, you may." Hope made herself at home, rummaging in the bathroom off the bedroom he shared with Clayton until she found the cup they used when brushing their teeth. If she noticed that only one of the beds in the room was rumpled and had far too many pillows for a single man, she didn't give any indication.

"If Little Miss Innocent here can trash talk around us, I figure it's only fair." He attempted to snatch the glass and pills from her but missed entirely. His vision had started to double and the resulting halo made him dizzy.

Two of Hope Compton was a hallucination he didn't mind.

Lustrous hair fell in rich chestnut waves to her waist. Her compact, dainty build made it hard to believe either Silas or Colby could be her father. The pretty almond eyes she focused on him were rimmed with thick lashes. And the ghost of her black eye.

The reminder of what had almost happened wrung his guts.

"Clay." The other man understood as always. He grabbed Wyatt when he lurched toward the bathroom and held him steady as he emptied his stomach. Again.

Right about the time he wished someone would be kind enough to put him out of his misery, he heard Hope's sweet voice in the background. "Mom, I need you."

Oh no. Another round of oily sickness assaulted him.

"Yes, please hurry. He's going to need something like cefazolin, I think. No, stronger. I'd give him the penicillin to start, but he's not going to be able to keep it down." A pause sealed his fate. "I think he's afraid of the hospital. Or it could be a financial thing. I'm not sure. There's no time to argue about it, though. Would Dr. Hill make a house visit? We owe Wy enough to call in some favors."

"You're all right now." Clay added to his humiliation by rubbing his back and hauling him up from where he'd melted into a heap. His partner wiped his face with a cool cloth and tried his best to soothe Wyatt. It worked. The guy always knew how to reach beneath the surface and calm his demons. Why should now be different?

"Thanks, Mom. See you soon. Love you too." Hope's phone beeped as she disconnected.

When Wyatt stumbled from the bathroom, leaning heavily on his other half, he didn't know what to say to the dark angel standing before him. She took away his uncertainty and bridged the gap for him. "Help is coming. Go ahead and try to get comfortable. I've got some iodine and cream to clean out the wound. I won't lie, it's going to hurt."

"More than it already does?" Clayton put himself between Wyatt and Hope.

"Yes. It'll be a little worse before it starts getting better. Sorry." She winced as she peeked at the mess his hand had become.

"I can handle it. Do what you have to. Quit talking. Start working." He collapsed into bed, ready to howl when the heavy hand flopped onto the quilt by his side.

"Be nice or I won't be gentle." Hope administered the iodine from one of those new pen-style dispensers that kept excess from pouring all over while targeting the area in need of sterilization.

"Mother fucker!" He arched off the bed. Or would have if Clay hadn't practically sat on him to keep him in place.

"And just so you know...my dad says you're suspended with pay until my mom gives you the all clear."

Wyatt didn't know if it was her decree or the next splash of healing fire that pushed him over his limits. Unnatural midnight crept closer until it claimed more than just the periphery of his vision.

"No, don't wake him. Let him slide under." A soft hand covered Clayton's large one on Wyatt's cheek. "It's better if he doesn't feel this. Let his mind protect him."

She couldn't know about the hell waiting in his dreams.

Clay whispered in his ear, "I'll be right here. You're safe."

The reassurance allowed Wyatt to sink below the surface of his consciousness.

Chapter Five

Clayton had tried his best not to pull his hair out in clumps while he watched Hope's mom rig Wyatt to a fancy IV infusion system. Once Dr. Hill arrived, it only got worse. Whatever they did must have been for Wyatt's own good. They wouldn't hurt the man. Still, his unconscious lover's groans drove Clay insane. He wanted to hold Wy. Whisper that he wasn't leaving no matter what. Except he couldn't. He didn't have that right. Not with this audience, and Wy's insistence that they keep their relationship quiet around work. Which was bullshit.

How much longer could he hide the enormity of his lust and admiration for his best friend? Why should he have to?

Clay marched from the room and plopped onto their hideous olive green couch. He'd never assessed the shabbiness of the revolting-yet-good-enough furniture until Compton royalty occupied his and Wyatt's private domain.

Spartan, sure. Functional, though. Homey and welcoming without extra frills.

The dilapidated cushion sank despite the slight weight that could only belong to Hope as she settled next to him. He didn't dare open his eyes. A man could only take so much torture before he lost his shit. "I know I should offer you something, but I'm pretty sure you're not into beef jerky and beer. Maybe a can of beans to round out the sides."

Ten tons of worry weighed Clayton down. He couldn't even lift his head from the cushion to read the disappointment he was sure he'd find on Hope's pretty face.

"That's not necessary. Really. Though you shouldn't assume you know what I like without asking. You might be surprised." She scooted closer and laid her tiny palm on his knee.

Maybe Wyatt was right. They'd hurt her if they weren't careful. If they didn't keep their distance. Considering the damage they'd done to Boone, neither looked forward to that kind of fallout in the near future. Or ever again.

Her sweetness wasn't helping to curb his appetite though.

"Actually..." Her daddy, Colby, joined them while Lucy finished up with Wyatt and her other husband, Silas, stood guard. "Hope should whip up some grub. She's a great cook, even when the pickings are slim. A warm meal might do you good. You look like hell, kid."

"Thanks, Foreman." Clay couldn't help his chuckle. At least he could trust the guy's word. He didn't try to sugarcoat stuff. "And, no. Your family has already gone to enough trouble."

"It's nothing," Hope volunteered. "Besides, I like to play around in the kitchen. This sounds like a challenge. You've got to eat. When's the last time you had something?"

His stomach rumbled its opinion on the matter. Good thing there was no way to measure the hunger inspired by the mental flash of Hope *playing around* in an apron with nothing beneath it. The foreman would deck him if he could read minds.

"See." Hope patted his leg then bounced off the uneven springs toward their kitchenette. "Great idea, Daddy."

Clay winced when Colby traded places with his daughter. The man's inscrutable stare unnerved Clayton. What if he could see thoughts after all? *Uh oh.*

"It's a hell of a lot harder to be the guy without control. The person watching while your partner suffers." The foreman kept his insights low enough to stay private while his daughter rummaged through barren cabinets, scavenging an assortment of imperishable odds and ends from the recesses of the pantry—some soup, a can of corn, half a bag of rice and who knew what else.

Neither he nor Wy had bothered to take up Boone's culinary slack after things had gone to shit. Right about the time Wyatt cracked and kissed a woman who'd practically assaulted him at their usual hangout, Spurs. It hadn't been Wy's fault, really. All three of them had known he couldn't go pussy-free forever. But it *was* another disaster Clay had been powerless to stop.

Taking the backseat for his entire life was starting to unravel him.

He scratched the thickening stubble on his chin. Shaving hadn't been a priority in the past twenty-four hours.

"I've spent enough time with you two to see you're too damn much like Silas and I were back before we knew better. Before Lucy broke through to him. It's gonna be okay, kid." Colby didn't relent. "Trust me. Hanging in there is worth it in the end. You'd have split by now if it wasn't the real thing. It might be fucked up, but it's there. You can work on it together. He'll admit to himself what you've got soon enough. Until then, you have to be the stronger man."

Clay refused to succumb to the burning behind his eyes. "How can you be so sure?"

The thick, heavy hand Silas Compton dropped on Clay's shoulder from behind the couch shocked him speechless.

"Because a man can only be a blind fool for so long when everything in the universe steers him toward his destiny." The cowboy cleared his throat, then moved past as if he'd said all he intended to on the subject.

A giant grin eroded Silas's intimidation factor a bit. He monitored Hope's ingenuity and the kind spirit his family had nurtured in her. The glance he tossed over his shoulder screamed his love and appreciation for the pair who'd been awfully patient with him if even a tiny fraction of the ranch legends were true.

Lucy rounded the sofa last, settling easily into her first husband's arms. "Wyatt's sleeping peacefully now. He'll be out for a long time. Don't let that frighten you. His body is fighting for him."

"He'll be okay?" Clay asked.

"Yeah. He's lucky you were here to get help. His hand will recover fully. The rest is up to him. And you. I know this look, Clayton." She surprised him by reaching over to kiss his cheek.

Even worse was Silas's grunt at the stare Hope shot them. Were those green sparks he caught in her eyes?

Clay couldn't restrain his curiosity another moment. "Did you really write a letter to Silas every day for ten years?"

"I'm persistent like that." She nodded and snuggled into Colby's chest.

For a second, Clay hated them. They had everything he needed so desperately. In a way the ranch, the land and the wealth they possessed never had, their intimacy riled something disgusting in him. The ugly thought turned to relief as he deliberately tamped bitterness from his soul, replacing it with joy that someone had found their greenest pasture.

But how much longer would he be able to win that fight against ingrained pessimism?

It got harder every day.

He was tired.

Fucking exhausted.

His lids fluttered closed.

"If it's ever too much, you can come talk to us. We understand." Colby's generous offer had him about to smile before he grimaced.

Not like he could reciprocate their openness. Especially since he envisioned Hope as the link he and Wy had been missing—the female touch Wyatt needed and he enjoyed.

"Thank you." Regardless of the unlikeliness of him taking them up on it, he worked hard to explain himself. "Since we came here, you've been damn good to us. Today. This. It's more than we could ever repay."

Lucy shushed him. "We don't keep score around Compass Ranch."

"But if we did, you'd still be miles ahead." Colby beamed as he watched their daughter with Silas.

Priceless, her innocence and the joy of life shone from within until it kind of hurt to look at her.

"Almost done." She turned to smile at him as the microwave counted final seconds to full temperature on her concoction.

"I think we should leave you to your dinner." Lucy rose. She tugged her husband along behind her.

Clayton appreciated them sparing him. Being an awkward spectacle as he ate the single serving of dinner didn't sit well with him. He only regretted that Hope would disappear with the trio of ranch leaders.

Silas joined his lovers, enfolding one of their hands in each of his. He nudged them toward the door as a unit while Hope used a threadbare towel to deliver Clayton's meal to the coffee table made of milk crates and an old board they'd found in the barn.

Fragrant steam drifted up from the modified stew.

"There's enough for you to have a second bowl." She wrung her hands in front of her waist. "If you like it. When you're done, pour the rest from the pot into your bowl and give it forty-five seconds in the ionizer."

He didn't bother to correct her. They still had an ancient microwave in the bunkhouse.

"Hope." Silas interrupted before Clay could reassure her he'd savor every drop because she'd bothered to make it for him. "Maybe you should stay."

Clayton's eyebrows climbed probably about as high as Hope's had.

"It's a good idea, honey." Colby smiled.

"You can keep an eye on Wyatt and feed this boy some more soup," Lucy joined in.

"But I don't have anything else to share." Clayton could kick himself for not taking the time to shop. Son of a bitch, it would have been nice to have some company. "Sorry. You'd be better off leaving."

"Nonsense." Lucy wouldn't hear of it. "I'll have Austin run over some supplies in a while, how about that?"

Hope turned radiant when her full-on smile graced her lovely face. Plump lips parted, making him think of naughty things. She trotted over to her parents then hugged and kissed them all, one by one. "Thank you. I love you so much."

She whirled toward Clay again, her hair turning into a soft silken sheet.

When she caught the emotion in his stare she paused, maybe mistaking it for reluctance instead of awe. "Unless..."

"No. I'd like that. A lot." He couldn't say what inspired him unless it was Silas and the way he'd done the same with his mates. Clayton held out his hand.

His Compass Girl nibbled her still-damaged lip before closing the gap between them.

Hope blushed when she looked at her parents. Her fingers linked with Clayton's as she perched on the arm of the sofa. Her mother nodded at her and smiled.

"Call us if you need anything." Her dad, Silas, made it clear with a single pointed glare that included ass-kicking.

"Bye." She wiggled her free fingers at her daddy, Colby, who took the hint. He opened the door and ushered them out. "Wow, sorry."

"If I had a daughter I'd do the same." Clayton rubbed the spot between her thumb and forefinger. "Especially if she was as adorable as you."

She shivered. "I appreciate them. I swear I do. But sometimes it's a little much. I'm probably the world's most sheltered twenty-three-year-old. I think part of the problem is that I'm still in school, so they don't think of me as out on my own. Well, that and the fact that I still sort of live at home. Maybe I should look at an apartment in town."

"No, don't. You like staying with your cousins, right?" He seemed genuinely interested. "I always see you four in the yard, laughing, smiling, joking, talking with your grandmother on the porch. Seems like you've been doing that more lately. I mean, not like I'm stalking you or anything. Just that..."

"I've seen you too." She smiled and touched his tense arm. Why did she keep doing that? And why did he keep letting her. "You ride really well. I love the way you handle the animals. Even the greenest horses let you close. More than any of the other cowboys. Sometimes they accept you even easier than my Uncle Seth."

"Yeah, it's a weird talent I've always had." He shrugged, then lapped up some more of her soup. She realized he was scraping the bottom of the bowl.

"Here, let me refill you."

"Thanks." He shot her a sheepish grin. "Um, do you want some for yourself?"

Hope laughed. "No, you go ahead. I'm good to hang on until my little brother shows up."

A groan snuck past her lips as she prepared the second helping, excited he'd liked it well enough to take more. Though, hungry as he was, it probably wouldn't have mattered what she set in front of him.

"What is it?" Clayton started to rise until she waved him off.

"Just that Austin is going to grill you." She shook her head. "He idolizes all the ranch hands, like Doug does. I'm sure they pester you enough at work."

"Nah. It's nice. Kind of fun." He patted the seat beside him so she joined him on the couch again. In between spoonfuls of stew, which he slurped greedily, he continued, "I wish I hadn't had to be so cynical when I was their age. Wyatt too. Some hero worship might have done us good."

"You didn't have any role models around growing up?" Hope wondered if he'd answer when he took several more swallows.

"No. We just had each other. Grown-ups weren't really trustworthy in our world. My mom and his dad hooked up when we were kids." He stared off out the window at the gathering dusk. "Mostly for drugs. I mean, on my mom's side of the bargain, anyway. His dad, well, he used her. I think he hoped my mom would take care of Wy and his sister. But she was so far gone after a while..."

Hope laid her head on Clay's shoulder. She rubbed the knots from his neck and shoulders with one hand, but didn't say anything. No words could heal his heart. Affection might though. Picturing the lonely, scared child he'd been, she attempted to infuse him with caring.

"Yeah. My mom didn't come home one time. We never heard from her again. Honestly, I know she OD'd. I guess the details aren't important."

Hope disagreed, but she didn't dare interrupt him.

"Wy's dad drank whenever he could afford another bottle. I'm not sure he even noticed when my mom died. Except that he was pissed he got stuck with three kids to feed. Then Wy's sister—" Clay seemed awfully interested in the pea he swirled around with his spoon. "Well, he and I split. I was twelve. He was thirteen. We got odd jobs and stole some until we could find something steady. Legitimate."

"I'm sorry." She hugged him then, giving up all semblance of distance between them. "That had to hurt your pride. You're an honorable guy."

"How would you know?" His huff annoyed her.

"Maybe because you risked your own ass for mine Monday night?" She growled when she realized he'd made her curse again.

"I guess there's that." Clayton dropped his spoon in the re-emptied bowl. While she peeked over her shoulder to glimpse Wyatt through the open doorway, still resting, Clay angled his knees toward hers until they bumped together. "But how do you know I wasn't being selfish? Maybe I wanted what they were about to take. Could be I'm tired of always putting everyone else's needs ahead of mine. When the hell is it my turn?"

"Right now." With her chin raised, she welcomed his advance. It might not be good manners to make out with another guy's boyfriend while he was injured in the next room.

But she considered the infraction temporary. Someday soon Wyatt would have a chance at the same. If he wanted it. Still, it might be best to check out her assumptions. "I mean, as long as that won't put you in a bad spot with your boyfriend. I don't know how things work between you."

"He and I have always been clear with each other. If there's a woman we're attracted to, we go for it. Sometimes that's been solo. Most times together. Gotta say, he'd be in my corner this time, no doubt. I've seen how he looks at you. Probably he'd call me a lucky bastard, but he wouldn't stop it."

"Then I stand by what I said. It's your turn. Right now. This time…take."

Clayton pounced.

They jiggled as the worn couch gave beneath their momentum. Hope welcomed Clay's weight and the press of his body, full-length, against hers. The storminess of his eyes had her reaching up, burying her fingers in his hair. It was as soft as she remembered.

"Hell, yes," he whispered before pouring himself into a kiss so full of desperation and aching tenderness that tears stung her eyes.

She'd never been kissed like this. With soft sweeps of his mouth and rough licks of his tongue over the seam of her lips. A gasp allowed him entrance and he took full advantage. Though urgent, she never would have called his sucks and nips selfish.

Hope gave Clay everything he asked for, all he wanted, and then some because what she needed was the same. A man who saw past the family name she carried and teased out the adventurous side lurking deep inside her. Gentle, yet fierce. Bold, yet careful.

Breath came in small pants that didn't do much for relieving the burning in her chest. She struggled to get closer to him and to find space to gasp for air. Her breasts mashed against his chest and the heavy slice of his arrowhead rested in the dip of her collarbone.

When he traveled from her mouth to her neck, she arched off the couch. His teeth sank into the skin beneath her ear just enough to make her whimper for more. The bend of her spine aligned them completely. Even through his jeans, there was no hiding his hardness beneath.

What should she do about it? Her hand roamed down his chest and cupped the bulge. Wonder coursed through her. So big. So rigid.

What would it feel like to have him inside her? She stiffened, a little fear mixing with her arousal and excitement.

Clay froze above her. They both blinked.

He reared back so fast he nearly knocked the cushion from the couch. "Whoa. What the—that got *way* out of hand. I'm sorry, Hope. I shouldn't have. We shouldn't."

"Because of Wyatt?" She pressed her fingers to her still-tingling lips. The taste of Clayton on her tongue was delicious. Thinking was nearly impossible when every system in her body was in full-steam-ahead mode although he'd already slammed on the brakes.

"Kind of. Maybe. I don't know." Clay tumbled to his ass on the far side of the couch. His legs ran parallel to hers. Hope mimicked him until the whole length of the seat guaranteed they couldn't molest each other again for the moment.

"There's a lot going on today." For her too. From nothing to everything in minutes. Powerful rushes of excitement and trepidation pulsed through her veins. It was scary. Almost like she had tried the drugs his mother had fallen victim to instead of an anything-but-simple kiss. And she wanted to do it again. Now. "Maybe I should go."

Hope glanced into the other room where Wyatt lay still beneath a layer of blankets she suspected he never otherwise used. He'd been so hot when she touched his feverish skin. Some of that came from within, not a byproduct of his system battling his infection.

She'd bet Clayton never went to bed cold.

How could she risk that bond for them? She hadn't had time to really talk to her mom. How did this work? What if she broke them apart? She'd never forgive herself.

"Please, don't." Clay rubbed the bridge of his nose. "Wyatt might need you."

"And you?" she wondered aloud, unafraid of being direct. No sense in being coy now.

"I need you too. Stay. We'll talk. Watch a movie. No more..." He swung his finger from his chest to hers and back. "I promise. I just—don't leave me alone tonight, please."

Shit. She wished he weren't so damn admirable. But it was for the best.

The instincts he employed every time he tamed one of the ranch horses had flared to life at her momentary hesitation. And when they settled next to each other again, their hands clasped tightly together, she knew he'd been right. Smarter than her. As the night wore on, she realized the closeness forming between them had more to do with who they were than the chemical reaction that lit her body on fire when they touched. Though that certainly didn't hurt.

And tomorrow they'd have to confess to Wyatt what they'd done. How they felt. Because she wasn't imagining the force with which the man beside her clung in return.

What they hell were they going to do now?

Chapter Six

Something disturbed Hope's doze. She burrowed deeper into the squishy bed and tried to ignore Daniel and whoever he argued with.

"You did what?" Wyatt's roar—not Daniel's—had her bolting upright. Not in her room or even her home. She oriented herself to the bunkhouse as the rumble of Clay's urgent persuasion added to her discomfort.

She wished she could hear what he said.

Was it an apology for what they'd shared? The places they'd touched still hummed with energy and happy tingles.

"You're only going to end up hurting her. You dumbass. Haven't you learned anything?"

More low, fast talking.

"I don't care if she kisses as good as she looks. No. And no again."

Elation mixed with hurt. Smug, she grinned hearing that she'd affected Clay. Vanity warred with the sting of rejection.

"It's never going to happen, Clay." Wyatt got so thunderous, she knew he was sending her a message.

Received. Loud and clear.

"Absolutely *never*."

Hope blinked away the tears gathering there. She refused to invest more of herself in an ungrateful asshole, even if he had a spectacular best friend. Enough of that nonsense had resulted in an epic failure with John.

After slipping on her sneakers, she slunk toward the clear Wyoming air and freedom from the pain Wyatt inflicted on her with every crushing syllable. Her fingers clenched the doorknob when Clay emerged from the bedroom.

"Shit, Hope. I'm so sorry you heard that." His face burned crimson. With rage or embarrassment, maybe both. "He didn't mean—"

"Quit making excuses for your asshole roommate." She shook her head. "You're lying to yourself and allowing him to bully you. At what cost, Clay? You may have a warm body to keep you company, but you're as lonely as I am."

She crossed to the man who'd chatted the night away with her. Hardly recognizable now, his eyes were shuttered and his easy familiarity had vanished.

"He'll come around." Clay swallowed hard.

"I deserve better than having to convince a cranky cowboy to be with me." She paused and stared into his sensual eyes, remembering how they had nearly glowed with suppressed passion last night. "So do you. You know where to find me if you wise up."

He flinched, his spine so stiff beneath her palms that she abandoned her embrace for fear of snapping him in two.

"Make sure he eats when he takes those pills. My mom will probably stop in at lunch to check on his progress. If you need help before then, call Dr. Hill. I left the number on the nightstand yesterday."

Her leaden feet required a lot of force to shuffle toward the exit. All her dreams had revolved around the promise of paradise she thought these charming walls contained.

"Hope, wait—"

She didn't.

A bang echoed through the house, likely caused by a man's fist, as she crossed the porch. She picked up steam, jogging toward home and the cousins who would convince her that her heart couldn't possibly be as bruised as her face after a single evening, a steamy kiss and one failed experimental walk, toeing the boundary of the wild side.

Hope pasted on a fake smile and entered the main house on the ranch, where Sunday dinner had already begun. Her dad and uncles had grown up here. They all still felt at home in the sprawling colonial. The Compass clan came and went as they pleased.

Delaying as long as possible, she'd fussed with her hair. An attempt to hide the damage to her cheekbone was prudent. Maybe not for vanity, as when she'd plotted to be at her most beautiful with Vivi earlier in the week. However, she didn't want any of her family members winding up in jail, so it was critical to minimize the proof of her pain. Plus, finding another outfit required more give-a-damn than she could muster.

Prettying up her outside hid some of the ugly negativity festering inside. It wasn't her style to mope around, all doom and gloom and crap. Hanging out with her family would break her from her slump if anything could.

The aroma of beef, roasted slow until tender, had her mouth watering at least half as much as Clay had yesterday. The stomp of her foot drew curious glances from a couple of her relatives. But damn it, she couldn't go more than ten seconds without recalling the laughter they'd shared over cheesy movies or second-guessing her refusal to call and check on Wyatt.

"You look awfully nice, Hope." Uncle Sam picked her up and whirled her around as if she hadn't yet graduated from elementary school. Honestly, she didn't mind. Carefree and joyous, those days held good memories. Ones she could lean on now. "Trying to impress somebody?"

Over his shoulder, she caught Aunt Cindi's wince in the mirror on the fireplace mantle along with the sawing action she drew over her throat as she attempted to subtly warn her husband off behind Hope's back.

"Guess I somehow put my boot in my mouth again, huh?" He chuckled.

"It's okay." She patted his chest as he set her down. "I'm kind of glad I'm not the talk of the Mothers. Surprised too."

"Well, I wouldn't say that." Aunt Leah laughed. "But maybe we haven't shared all the gritty details with the Compass Brothers. You know how they get about their girls."

"I do." She rushed into the kitchen to help Vivi before her uncles could demand an explanation.

Surprised, she drew up short when she found Boone taking a lighthearted slap from her grandmother. The thin guy sported a frilly apron over what probably constituted his entire wardrobe of dress shirts.

When he caught her tight smile, he paused with a peach cobbler clasped between mismatched potholders, halfway to the open oven.

"Come on, get it in there." Vivi laughed. "*That's what she said.* Again."

Oh my God. "Vivi!"

"Don't be such a prude, girly." Her grandmother's peal of giggles did a lot to lighten Hope's heart. "That's an oldie but a goodie. Surprised Jake knew it. Haven't heard it in years."

Boone looked to Hope but didn't correct the older woman. Jake was even older than her dads. Certainly not one of the younger generation of ranch workers, though he still had a place of honor in their ranks. If he wasn't already in the living room watching TV with her uncles, he would be soon. Would that confuse Vivi even more?

Crap, it was getting harder to mask the slips lately.

Hope crossed to the sink and began to wash her hands. Boone joined her, with one lean hip propped against the counter and his back turned to her grandmother, who now mashed potatoes vigorously. Frown lines marred her classic beauty.

"Hey." He nodded.

"Hi." So many questions piled up in her throat that none could break free.

"You doing okay?"

"Clay told you about this morning?" She frowned.

"Um, no. I was talking about the last time I saw you, when you got slightly beat up." He wiggled his fingers toward her shoulder and her face. "But now I want to know about that."

"Oh." Hope glanced at Vivi, who seemed preoccupied with vaporizing the potatoes, then the rest of her relatives, who were all busy with their own conversations. "Let's just say words can hurt a hell of a lot more than fists sometimes."

"I don't know why Clay lets Wyatt open his mouth other than... Well, yeah. Not for talking." Boone grimaced.

How well he knew them to have gotten things that close to the bull's eye. She couldn't resist another second.

Hope laid her hand in the crook of Boone's elbow and hauled him toward the tiny foyer near the front door. No one used the formal entrance much. "What happened between you guys? Spill and I'll do the same."

"A trade. Nice." Boone sighed. "Long story short, Wyatt is bisexual. Actually, I'm pretty sure he's mostly straight. Except for Clay. Though I don't think he's ever admitted he's head over heels in love with the man. Either to himself or to Clayton. It's bullshit."

"I noticed he's a little...unavailable. Emotionally." She thought back on the terror in his eyes at the bar. More than her close call warranted.

"You could put it that way if you want to be nice." Boone stared at the floor. "Basically, he didn't like how close Clay and I were getting. So he sucked face with some bar chick where I'd find them. He told me he couldn't do without occasional pussy and that things just weren't going to work out. I swear he knew I'd get jealous after a while. That I'd break it off. He was protecting Clay."

"I'm sorry. Do you regret it?" Hope patted his shoulder even as a wave of envy assaulted her.

"No. It stings. Not going to say it doesn't. But it wouldn't have worked. He was right to kill it early. I wouldn't have been able to handle them bringing girls around or the ghosts haunting him into locking his feelings away."

Perfect. "Tell me about his sister."

"Wow. You're smart. Took me months to figure out that was the problem." Boone sighed. "She's dead."

Blood leached from Hope's face. What would she do if something happened to Austin? Or one of her cousins? It would tear her world apart. How could she blame Wyatt for that?

"How?"

"His dad. Flew into a drunken rage. Something Wy had done. A minor infraction. She covered for him and took the heat. Wyatt's dad probably didn't mean to shove her down the stairs. Broke her neck. Over quick. Nothing to be done." Boone got kind of pissed when he noticed the tears in her eyes. "Not you too. Don't cut him any slack for ancient history. Look, I feel bad for Wy and that poor girl. Honestly. But let it go already. Hasn't that one horrible tragedy ruined enough of his damn life? It's going to destroy Clayton's too."

"Let me be the judge of that." A rich tenor had Hope's insides simultaneously melting and steeling.

"Clay." Boone pivoted to face the new arrival.

When Hope peeked up to measure just how pissed he was, she got a real shock. Wyatt stood beside his friend, his complexion so gray she thought he might pass out. "What the hell are you doing out of bed?"

Nothing she'd heard from Boone made her change her course. She darted to Wy's side, reaching onto her tiptoes to press her palm to his forehead. Warm yet not the inferno he'd been yesterday.

"I don't take commitments lightly," he answered without flinching from her touch. "I said I'd be here. And I wanted to talk to you. About this morning."

"Later." Hope refused to put his health last. How often had he taken care of those around him to his own detriment?

"Not even going to argue, big guy?" Boone's eyes widened. "You must be feeling shitty. Come on."

Sweat dotted Wyatt's brow. He allowed his two fellow cowboys to flank him, each with a hand on his arm, subtly holding him up as he weaved into the family room and tumbled onto a vacant loveseat.

"Hey, Lucy." Daniel already acted like family. He shouted over the projector and the Compass Boys wrestling on the floor in front of the digital screen. "You've got a patient over here."

"I'm fine, jackass." Everyone ignored the grumble from Wyatt. "Shut your mouth or I'll assign you to mucking stalls for the next three months."

"Sure, sure." Daniel waved him off. With Sienna perched on his lap and his fingers wandering through her hair, he didn't seem bothered by much. "Can't be a dick to me if you're dead, can you?"

Doug, Sienna's little brother, popped his head up. His ears tuned to Daniel like a drone locked on a heat signature. "That's a dollar for the curse jar. If I can't, you can't. Remember?"

Sienna chuckled. "You're going to be broke soon."

"Sorry for your luck, sunshine." Daniel fished a bill out of his wallet and handed it to the youngest Compass Boy.

Hope's mom barreled around the corner. "Wyatt! Did I say anything about getting out of bed in my instructions?"

"No, ma'am." At least he stared at his polished boots as he responded.

Hope tried not to allow her gaze to wander. No use. It traveled up his dark jeans, complete with a crease from being pressed, to the bulge just below his ornate belt buckle. The arrowhead in the middle caught her attention. She flicked a glance to Clay, who gnawed his lip.

Though she didn't have X-ray vision to spy the necklace he wore, she knew it was there because the cord lay against the tanned skin of his neck. Right where she'd clutched him last night as she drew him to her tighter.

She coughed, choking a little at the memory.

Boone tapped her between her shoulder blades.

"Thanks." A blush heated her cheeks.

"Anytime," he whispered, leaning close enough that the din in the house disguised his comments. "They're potent enough for an expert. A beginner like you... Good luck."

Over the next several minutes, Wyatt convinced Lucy he might as well stay rather than exert himself trekking home. Young and resilient—or possibly just infinitely stubborn—he'd taken bigger strides than any of them could have guessed in healing. Enough antibiotics for one of the bulls pumped through his system. That probably didn't hurt either.

Then dinner was ready. Silence lasted about ten seconds as everyone stuffed themselves full of Vivi's home cooking. Better every time.

Hope tasted nothing. Her appetite had less to do with savory dishes and everything to do with the sweet dessert she'd love to make of Clay and his cantankerous bunkmate. If Wyatt's unflinching regard was any indication, he felt the same way. So why had he chased her away?

He leaned across Clayton to growl at her.

"Soon is coming quickly." He didn't blink as he ordered, "We're going to have a chat. The three of us."

"We'll see." Hope refused to cow to his demands. It didn't sound like he'd changed his mind. Screw him. To dismiss her then demand an audience as if he were a king instead of a ranch hand—she didn't think so. Especially not to grind in his rejection.

Taking advantage of his relative immobility, she cleared dishes from the table.

In the kitchen, Vivi gave Hope two thumbs up. "Your boys are great. Polite and fierce. I like the way Colby helps Silas without stealing his dignity. They're a good fit for each other and for you. Go for it, girly."

"Thanks." She tried not to shudder at her grandmother's mistakes. Both regarding her exploded-on-take-off relationship and the use of her fathers' names. Gross and frightening that her grandmother had started mixing up her own sons instead of just the longtime hands.

Hope was going to have to talk to the rest of the Compass Girls soon.

But not right then.

Because at that instant, Sterling rounded the corner. "Your dickhead ex is out on the porch. Which of our dads do you want me to send out there to chase him off?"

"What? John?" The night kept sliding deeper into crapola land.

"That's the one. Assmuncher." Sterling cracked her knuckles. "Better yet, let me explain to him how a twatwaffle like him isn't welcome around here ever again."

"No!" Hope craned her neck to verify Wyatt and Clay were still embroiled in guy talk. Well, Clay was. Wyatt sat silent and watchful. Part illness, she figured. But also just the man he was. An observer. Content to sit on the sidelines of the commotion and soak it all in. Like her dad. Her head throbbed with all she had to consider. "I've got this. I have some things I'd like to say. Let me close that wound, Sterling."

Her cousin shrugged. "If you have to. Just don't take forever or I *will* send your dads."

"Five minutes." Hope nodded, then ducked through the throng. She slipped out the porch door, careful not to slam the screen door. Vivi would have shrieked at her if she had.

John leaned against his boring beige sedan. She remembered being impressed that he didn't drive a pickup like every other guy she knew. The women too, for that matter. With his hands jammed into the pockets of his lightweight windbreaker, he hunched forward. Poor posture didn't dissuade her from thinking that he looked small.

Compared to Clayton, and especially Wyatt, he was just an overgrown kid. And barely that. How had she been so dumb?

She'd assumed he was safe because he wasn't threatening. Being with a man so weak, in character more than body, had nearly cost her. Hope promised herself she'd never make that mistake again.

"Hope." He held his arms open.

Let them stay empty for all she cared. No way would she allow herself to be surrounded by him ever again.

"What do you need, John?" She put her hand on her hip and tossed her hair out of her eyes. The light from the barn must have illuminated her face.

"Oh, jeez." He hung his head. "I'm so sorry. Things got out of hand the other night, baby."

"Don't call me that." Her command snapped out. "And you're right, they did. I should never have let you push me into going—into believing your behavior lately was harmless."

"I shouldn't have cared what the guys thought of me. But what made you say...what you did?" He stared at her like she'd grown three heads. She supposed he had a right to feel that way to some degree. At no time had she given him any indication of the mustang running free inside her soul. She'd kind of thought the right man would recognize and tame it.

Well, maybe he would. They would.

"This isn't going to get us anywhere, John."

"Then come to my place. We can talk. And maybe see about trying some things. You're only dreaming about crazy stuff because you don't have any experience yet." He acted like the insanity he spouted was rational.

"You think I'd have sex with you? Ever? After what happened the other day?" She took a step back, and he advanced. The hairs on her arms stood on end.

Twisted laughter rolled over her lip, which still bore a faint crack. "Get out of here. And don't come around again. We're through. There's no chance I'll ever take you back."

Wyatt's similar declaration rang through her mind and stabbed her in the heart.

"I could make it so good for you. You wouldn't want another guy," John promised.

"I seriously fucking doubt that." Wyatt's snarl came from a few feet behind her. Not from her imagination this time. And Clayton's matching warning reverberated from her other side.

"Are you into pain, fucker?" The cold side of Clayton flashed out, surprising her once more with its efficiency. He might be quick to laugh, but he was faster to defend the people he prized. "We don't like to fight, but we'll kick your ass again if we need to reinforce our message."

"Stay away from Hope." Any lingering sickness had fled without a trace. Wy approached with the feral grace of a jungle cat.

"You got what you wanted, didn't you?" John went from scared to nasty when cornered. "That's why you're not interested in me anymore. You spread your legs for these two. And how many others? Maybe Damon was right—"

He didn't have a chance to finish because Clayton strangled him with a grip around his collar as he slammed the loser up against his own car.

"Stop." Hope stepped between the men despite Wyatt's grab for her. She reached Clay in time to prevent him from doing something he'd regret later. For her.

The fingers she blanketed with her own trembled. “He’s not worth it, Clay.”

“You are.” He took his eyes off John for a second to peer at her in the starlight.

John seized the opportunity to squirm free and bolted for his car. “You’re fucking nuts. All of you. You know what, fine. Have her. I don’t want your leftovers anyway.”

“No woman would settle for you after having a real man.” Wyatt shot John the finger as he slammed his car in reverse and peeled from the yard, spouting a rooster tail of gravel and dust.

As Hope gawked, a warm, gentle hand descended on the small of her back. Despite the fact that Wyatt spanned most of her torso with his palm, he didn’t frighten her or revolt her like John had. She allowed him to guide her into the barn. Clayton slid the giant door closed behind them, then flipped on a soft light in the tack room, providing enough of a glow that she could discern the apprehension in both cowboys’ faces.

If she wasn’t completely clueless when it came to them, she’d say there was a healthy bit of desire mixed in too. Did they plan to stake a claim instead of chasing her away?

She prayed they did.

Chapter Seven

"Are you insane?" Wyatt shouted at her before kicking a hay bale.

"He could have hurt you," Clayton murmured as he approached.

"Boone's big fucking mouth means you must know what that does to me." Wy rubbed his chest. "There were a million people in that house who love you and you'd risk yourself like that? For what? I know I'm fucking uncivilized sometimes, like this morning—not my best showing, I admit it—but being so inconsiderate of the pain you could have caused your family...that's just plain selfish and rude. Stupid."

When he put it like that, she shifted from foot to foot. "I wasn't afraid of John. I just wanted him gone. Permanently. And maybe to show him that he couldn't touch me, not really."

"But he *could* have." A vein stood out in Wyatt's neck, making her worry he'd over exert himself. Relapsing would prolong his recovery and stress him out. None of them needed that. Clay especially, since he had to live with Wy.

"One scream would have rained down enough angry cowboys on him to hold their own rodeo. Sterling knew what was going on and she's one of the best shots around." Security at Compass Ranch was guaranteed, in her mind. Nowhere else could have been as safe a haven for her. Unless it was in the arms of two loving ranch hands.

"No kidding, how do you think we realized what you were up to? You're lucky your father didn't notice her staring out the window. Hope—" Wyatt's persistence in his beliefs made her realize civil discussion wasn't an option. Maybe it never had been. A man like him respected action and bluntness over diplomacy.

Invoking the platinum rule, she prepared to treat him as he preferred.

A sudden fury ignited a conflagration in her like the lightning bolt that had struck the south hay field after last year's summer-long drought. In this case, the dearth turning her insides to kindling had lasted more than two decades, she supposed. "You know what? Shut the hell up. I've had enough of men deciding my future. My dads, my uncles, my ex-boyfriend and now you guys. You can suck it. If you don't want anything to do with me, you have no right to say how I live my life. A week ago you barely knew my name. Son of a bitch. You were half-dead yesterday and now you're going to come in here and start brawling to defend my honor or punish me for giving that dirt bag a piece of my mind? I don't need a shitty lecture from you. Save your energy."

Wyatt's grin spread slow and wide. "You cursed. A bunch."

"Fuck you!"

"Hope, you're wrong about one thing. We've known all about you for a while. How could we not?" Clayton's quiet honesty cut through her rage. "You stand out."

"You think we didn't see you prancing around here?" Wyatt scoffed. "We noticed you plenty."

"Then what the hell were you waiting for? Even after you found out I was curious about trying out your lifestyle, you didn't make me any offers. Damn it, I practically gave you an engraved invitation and you *declined.*" Allowing him to see her cry was out of the question. "So go home. Rest. Do the smart thing for once in your life."

Wyatt ignored her rant. He stared at her as if he actually considered what she'd shouted.

Crossing her arms, she refused to retreat.

"I get wanting to be in control of your destiny. I can respect independence. So is that all you need? To test drive two guys? Doesn't matter who?" Wyatt peered into her eyes as he put it on the line. "Will screwing us delete this ridiculous idea of the three of us together from your big brain? If you want to fuck, we can handle that. If you want more, it's impossible. Look at Boone. I won't do that to another person. And I certainly won't make you a target for ignorant fucks like the guys at the bar, who'd assume you'd be up for playing with them. Hiding in the shadows isn't any way to live either. You don't know what you're asking for. I didn't think you were the kind of woman who could separate emotion from sex, but I didn't think a lot of things about you. I like being wrong sometimes. Maybe this is one of those rare instances."

Something in her chest fluttered at his adaptability. Could she have judged him wrong too? Was he somewhat more flexible than she'd given him credit for? Steel instead of stone.

If he was bluffing, he was about to be sorry.

"Glad you're comfortable with fucking up because I think you're an expert by now." She loved how she could blurt exactly what she thought without polite phrasing and he could take it. Heck, he seemed to revel in their passionate exchange, which grew more vibrant by the instant.

Arguing with him, debating their future, did something wicked to her.

Hope took a step closer, tilting her head up to maintain eye contact. The intensity of his stare sliced through her, deep into her core.

"You're pushing him, sweetheart." Clay's nostrils flared like one of the horses when it scented a potential mate. "Me along with him."

Wyatt met her halfway. He caged her between himself and his bunkmate. Their powerful bodies formed canyon walls. She loved being trapped by them. Every instinct she possessed sang with the rightness of it. Surrounded by the two men—their heat and their scent—she feared she might beg them to teach her about all the things she could sense lying barely outside her reach.

"Serves you right." She pouted just a little.

"Why?" Clay tipped his head. "What'd I do?"

"You've been doing the same to me. Teasing me. Putting all these damn ideas in my head. Turning me on with no way to relieve the ache. Don't leave me like this." She tossed his words from last night in his face and sealed the deal.

"I won't. I—I can't." Clayton swallowed hard. He looked to Wyatt quickly before he tipped her head up and covered her mouth with his.

Exactly as it had the day before, the connection of their bodies sparked a reaction more potent than the electrostatic attraction that bonded the compatible compounds she'd studied so hard. With Clay, everything was covalent. They agreed on so much. Their personalities had made last night's companionship easy and light. Wyatt—opposite, and ionic. An explosion of magnetic energy. Or maybe the three of them could fuse into an archetypical bent bond.

Any case provided a similar outcome. A single, perfect connection.

Organic chemistry had never seemed sexy during her late nights of studying pharmacology. Hopefully they'd be up for some cram sessions as she learned her way around their bodies. Extra tutoring could be necessary. Whatever it took to pass their tests. She'd always been one hell of a student.

"What do you think you're doing?" Wyatt rasped. Though he probably intended to yell, the question came out as more of a strangled grumble.

"Kissing." Hope mumbled between the nibbles of their mouths on each other. Clay tasted as sweet and spicy as she remembered. "He's fucking good at it."

"He can't be that great if you're still able to talk. Or think, for that matter." Wyatt leaned in closer.

Shocked, she lost the ability to respond when the bulky guy cradled her head in one palm and his boyfriend's in the other. He held them both tenderly as he traced the intersection of their lips with the tip of his tongue. Pulling back long enough to smile and hum, he rejoined them. This time fusing them more completely in a three-way kiss.

Instead of fading out, the excitement and arousal pinging between them seemed to pump him up. Apparently sex acted like a super-drug on Wyatt's immune system. Because before she realized it, his hand had wandered along her nape. It roamed across the deep-cut back of her flirty dress. The dip made it clear she'd had to leave her bra in her well-stocked lingerie drawer.

A gasp separated her from the guys. They took the opportunity to collide with each other in a more urgent exchange that left her as breathless as their seduction of her lips. With an excellent vantage point she stared, entranced as the pair expressed their joy at homecoming and reconnecting with each other.

Fighting had strained them too.

"This is what you want? And Hope?" Wyatt growled before claiming his mate once more.

Clay groaned his response.

Had she done that to them? Instilled them with a little of the thrilling uncertainty racing through her veins along with a massive dose of lust? A tinge of unease infiltrated her hunger. When she would have leaned back—a tiny bit—to take a deep breath of fresh air not polluted with their pheromones, Wyatt pressed between her shoulders, reintroducing her to the mix.

This time they alternated. Clayton nuzzled her cheek while Wyatt bestowed his first solo kiss. She could hardly think of it as something that sounded so tame when he ravaged her. It was as if all the cells in her brain lit up, endorphins painting gorgeous pictures behind her scrunched lids.

Relief had her practically climbing him. Her already crazy attraction amplified with him in the mix. But it also held between them alone. No one was the third wheel here. With her parents, everyone was equal. It seemed the same for her, Wyatt and Clay.

Amazing.

He nipped her bottom lip carefully, then licked the spot that had split beneath the force of Damon's knuckles. Resting his forehead on hers, he pulled his chin away enough to say, "I should have hit him harder. Maybe stomped on his nuts. I don't want you to get hurt. Never again."

"I won't tell anyone about us," she promised.

"Not even your cousins?" Wyatt peered directly into her eyes.

"Don't take the Compass Girls away from her." Clay came to her aid. "This could be confusing. She might need someone other than us to talk to. Don't assume all the danger comes from outside. You remember what it was like for us at first, right?"

Wyatt hesitated.

"They all adore her parents. It won't be any different accepting Hope's desires." Clay approached behind his partner and laid his cheek on the bigger man's shoulder. "Plus, if Daniel is in the know he can keep an eye out at their place."

"Fine," Wyatt snapped. "Those four. No one else. Your grandmother was already asking a lot of questions tonight. Other people will suspect if we're not careful."

Hope wasn't sure she liked being their dirty little secret. The tension in Wyatt's chest made it clear he didn't plan to budge on this point, though. She placed her hands over his firm pecs, kneading them like one of her Aunt Cindi's barn cats when it mauled the blanket-lined box it lived in.

Still, Wy held himself rigid and aloof.

"I promise. I won't climb the ridge in the south pasture and scream what great lovers you are. Too bad for your reputations. And your egos." Not that either needed any inflating.

"Good girl." The calm before the storm vanished. Wyatt directed Clayton. "Carry her to the empty stall in the corner. Get her dress off."

"Now don't you wish you'd fixed that hand before it went haywire?" Clay made her giggle when he *tsked* at Wyatt. "You're going to miss out on untying those pretty laces and working her panties down her sexy legs. Do you think we'll find a thong under that skirt? Or maybe boyshorts. Something ruffly."

"Um." Hope bit her cheek. She prayed they wouldn't be disappointed.

Wyatt and Clay exchanged a heated stare as if they guessed the truth. By tacit understanding, they moved as one. Clayton scooped her into his arms and toted her toward the rear of the barn, away from the door and the light. She couldn't believe she was going to become part of the ranks of people who'd gotten ultra-lucky in this familiar place.

Once, when he hadn't realized Hope had been standing behind him, Jake had bragged that the barn had seen more action than a whorehouse. The ranch hand had become a staple in Compton Pass over the past several decades. A good friend of her fathers and Silas's brothers, he had become an honorary uncle. He treated her as much like a princess as the rest of the Compass clan. Ugh.

These young cowboys had no similar predilections. A welcome relief.

Wyatt snagged a horse blanket off one of the racks as they passed by. He draped it over the loose, fresh hay on the floor before Clayton laid her on the makeshift bed then followed her to the ground.

"You're so damn pretty, Hope." He trailed a knuckle over the arch of her brow. "I'm honored that you'd consider us to give you your first ménage. Or even to touch you at all. We're just two regular guys. You're..."

She didn't bother to correct him or his assumptions. Instead she answered as honestly as she could. "I didn't have a choice. This feels right. In a way it never has with anyone else."

"To me too." The soft press of his lips to hers lulled her.

"*Us* too." Wyatt cleared his throat. "So why does she still have that dress on?"

"I got distracted," the man covering her replied. Clayton tucked against her from head to crotch before her thighs parted around the thick trunks of his legs.

"No kidding." The stern tone from the leader of their trio had Hope's pussy slicking, preparing for the rest of his instructions.

She had passed ready several days ago. No doubt in her mind. Except for one thing...

"Guys, I didn't expect this tonight. I didn't think you were coming to dinner. Wyatt especially." She blushed as she considered the surprise they were about to get. Okay, so maybe she'd thought about dropping by their bunkhouse with leftovers after the family gathering had finished. And serving up some dinner in bed.

"What are you saying, Hope?" Wyatt cut to the chase.

"I'm not on birth control and I don't have any condoms with me. Hell, this dress doesn't exactly have pockets." She winced.

"Don't worry, we're covered," Wyatt assured her. "We both got Vasalgel-ed."

Hope laughed. "I didn't know it was a verb, but good to know. The polymer they inject into the vas deferens is supposed to be a hundred-percent effective. There hasn't been a single reported failure since the clinical trials in India during the early two-thousand-teens."

"It's kind of hot when you get nerdy like that." Wy used his undamaged hand to rub the bulge in his jeans.

"I prefer to call it smart, but thanks." She smiled. Until Clay's exploring fingers had her eyes rolling back in her head and a whimper replacing her amusement. They tracked up the length of her legs, toying with the hem of her dress before lifting it.

And revealing that her panties matched her bra. Non-existent. Bare, her engorged flesh was soothed by the breeze swirling around her in the barn even as she responded to the two men driving her wild and to what they were likely to do to her.

"You planned to seduce us?" Clay leaned in for another kiss, interrupting his grilling. He slipped his hand between her legs, groaning when his palm cupped naked, slick flesh. "Are you sure you're ready for this?"

"If I only wanted to talk, I would have worn underwear." She thrust her pelvis at him. "Hurry up already. Unless you're not a fan of women going commando?"

"I like that just fine. As long as you assumed it was me that was coming to dinner." Clayton grinned and nipped the edge of her answering smile.

Wyatt nodded. For a second, Hope thought he might leave them to each other. She silently dared him to run. Some of her determination must have flashed in her eyes because he laughed softly. "Have it your way."

He yanked the button fly of his jeans with his good hand, then shoved the pants that had framed his ass perfectly to the ground. With a kick, he rid himself of his boots. Finally, he stepped out of his clothes. The seams of his soft cotton shirt objected when he whipped it from his torso with a single off-center yank.

Hope nearly choked on the tongue Clay had slipped into her mouth to thrill the sensitive nerve endings in her palate and gums.

"Gorgeous, isn't he?" Clayton peeked over his shoulder as if the sight of his lover could never get old. She bet it wouldn't.

"Yeah." She squirmed beneath Clay, wishing she could see his matching bronze skin and the underlying muscles that shaped it into little hills and valleys as tantalizing as Wyatt's.

As if he could read her mind, Wyatt said, "Show off for the lady, Clay. Let her see what all that manual labor does for your body."

Wyatt knelt beside them. He grabbed Clayton's ass before settling near her. Together, they watched as the taller, thinner of the two guys discarded first his shirt then his jeans. How he got rid of them and his boots so quickly remained a mystery. Lithe twists of his torso and impressive strength allowed him to contort his frame in ways that could only be a benefit to kinky sex.

Their nudity eased her discomfort over being stripped from the waist down. In fact, she writhed, trying to haul her dress over her head so she could glide against them skin-on-skin. Ever helpful, Clayton slipped the floral painted-silk over her head. Before her shoulders could meet the blanket again, Wyatt cupped the breast nearest him.

"You have a killer rack." It seemed no one had ever told him staring was rude.

In this case, his undivided attention made her feel more like a goddess than a freak. "Not proportional."

She'd despaired over finding clothes that weren't too big in the waist if they accommodated her bust.

"Mmm. I'd say the ratio of plump tits to tiny waist is perfect." Clay measured her with a heated gaze before treating her other breast to a caress similar to the one bestowed by his partner. Their touches had a lot in common. Yet if she closed her eyes, she'd know which man was which without doubt.

Wy didn't take any prisoners. He went straight for her nipple and rolled it in his palm, hardening the tip until she found it difficult to breathe through the pleasure. Clayton took a more scenic route, pressing on the soft skin and drawing designs on the mound, which heightened her awareness of his touch. He encouraged her to wonder where he'd venture next then drew out a sigh of delight with his decision.

Before she had really gotten enough of their delicious manipulation, they'd descended in unison, applying the heat and moisture of their mouths to the job.

When Wy moaned against her breast, her spine arched, feeding him more of her chest.

"You taste good, Hope." Clay rubbed her tummy. If he planned to calm her, it didn't work. Instead, he inflamed her. Her fingers tunneled into their hair, holding them close even as she prayed for them to advance—to take this fantasy one enormous step farther.

"She smells even better." Wyatt scented the air like one of the stallions she'd seen in the pasture. "You going to do the honors? Warm her up, Clay. I know how good you are with that mouth."

"Would you like that?" Clay's eyes darkened, his pupils dilating until she caught her expression in their reflection. She looked every bit as desperate and urgent as she felt.

"Yes." She pushed on his shoulder, guiding him lower, though she couldn't have budged him if he weren't willing—hell, already in motion. "Please."

"You beg so nicely, Hope." Wyatt dragged his fingertip around her nipple then up her neck to her mouth. He inserted it between her lips.

With them, nothing seemed forced. She did what felt right and their hungry stares proved it to be the perfect thing. They made it easy to experiment. She sucked on his finger, liking the way he filled her mouth.

"It's been a long damn time since we were with a woman who didn't seem fake." Clayton hovered over her mound. He nuzzled the apex of her thighs before breathing deeply. "I love how natural you are. How honestly you share your passion. Let me return the favor."

Hope lost suction on Wyatt's finger when her jaw dropped open.

An amused rumble drew her attention to Wy. "I wasn't joking. Clay's damn fine at servicing his partners. And he loves to do it too. Don't you?"

She picked her head up long enough to spy the red-hot stare Clay winged to Wyatt before he dove into his treat. *Her.* The rap of her skull on the lightly cushioned surface below her returned some clarity to her mind.

"Here." Wyatt urged her to lift again. He wadded his T-shirt beneath her nape, supporting her while improving her view. "Let him know when he does something you like so he'll do it more. Simple, right?"

Good thing. Complex reasoning went out the window about the time he licked her slit from end to end, concentrating several swirls around her engorged clit. She didn't need Wy's coaching to call out then. Her pussy clenched. Wetness spilled from her.

Clay was quick to lap it up.

"Save some to ease the way." Wyatt's gruff joke held a note of seriousness. "You're not exactly small, you know."

"Look who's talking." Clay paused long enough to wink at her. "You can peek. We don't mind."

She couldn't believe she hadn't checked them out. But honestly, she'd been dazzled enough by the heat in their eyes and the ultra-fit tone of their chests and abs to short-circuit her brain. With their permission, she followed the length of Wyatt's torso downward. He rolled onto his back, using her breast to pillow his head.

"Go ahead. Touch me." He made it sound as if he were granting her access, not as if he were aching for her hand on his cock. The full erection he sported had her nibbling her lip. Could he really fit inside her?

Growing up on a farm left her no doubt as to the mechanics of sex and the seeming impossibility of some biological phenomena. It'd never been her parts in question before, though. Wyatt clasped her hand in his good one and flattened it against his chest. The pounding of his heart reassured her in some twisted way.

He slid their joined fingers down his torso, allowing her to read the ridges of his abs like Braille that declared him sinfully sexy. And then she encountered steely flesh beneath soft skin. The contrasting textures fascinated her. When Clayton redoubled his efforts, apparently as excited by watching them play as she was by the wriggling of his tongue, she closed her fist around Wyatt harder than intended.

He grunted and she let go as if burned.

"That wasn't a sound of pain." His laughter came tight and rough. "Get your hand back here. Stroke me. Not too fast. Just enough. Make me good and hard."

"Mission accomplished." She tested his stiffness again. Yep, firm.

Clayton kissed her clit before whispering, "That's not all he has to offer. I think he's still hurting a little even if he's not letting on. Make him forget about being sick, Hope. Give him something better to focus on."

Wonder infused her every caress as she noted him solidifying and growing beneath her gentle pulls. If he got any bigger he really would be enormous.

"What kind of guys have you been with that you're looking at me like that?" Wy angled his head toward hers for a deep, drugging kiss that prohibited her from admitting her inexperience.

But it didn't take long for Clayton to discover and divulge her secret.

As she and Wy devoured each other and her hand pumped faster, Clay snuck the tip of a finger into her pussy. He rasped, "Damn, she's tight."

"Work her open." Wyatt barked between kisses. "You'll take her first. You're not as thick."

"But longer," Clay defended his manhood. Literally.

Hope giggled, though Wyatt swallowed the light sound. Along with her gasp when Clayton nudged something that sent a zing of unpleasant sharpness along with the bubbles of ecstasy he manufactured with his skilled handling.

"Wyatt." Clay turned still and serious between her legs.

"Don't screw around." The big cowboy grew more urgent by the second, riding her hand now, thrusting his hips up to meet her shuttling fist. "It's been too long. She's too sweet."

"Wy," he repeated. This time more firmly.

All three of them paused.

"What?" Wyatt's impatience seeped into his snarl.

"Come here." Clay curled his finger, making her imagine the internal massage he'd been attempting to give her just moments ago. She wished he'd shut up and get back to it.

"Are you kidding?" Wyatt pressed one last kiss to her lips, then to her breast before joining his roommate. "I thought you'd mastered finger-fucking in like fifth grade. You need help all of a sudden?"

"Shut up, asshole." The more sensitive of the two fought back. "Feel this."

Clay took hold of Wyatt's good hand, then guided his friend's index finger to Hope. She suddenly imagined she was the subject of a bizarre examination or maybe an alien abduction when Wyatt probed her while his partner looked on.

From here she confirmed neither of them had lost their hard-ons. That had to be a good sign. A deep exhalation followed her relief. The relaxation of her muscles allowed Wyatt to tunnel deeper. Again the stab of pain flashed between her legs when he attempted to burrow into her channel.

"You're a virgin?" Wyatt reared back.

"Hope?" Clay climbed her body. He settled beside her, gathered her to his chest and caressed the side of her face when she didn't answer right away. "It's okay. You know, if you are. We don't want to hurt you. Be honest."

"I've been riding horses my whole life." Her gaze darted around the room as she avoided looking at the two bulky men above her. Humiliation set her cheeks on fire. "Jade promised you wouldn't be able to tell."

"I damn well can feel there's never been a man past this point." Wyatt kneaded the barrier she hadn't known she possessed. "Look at me, Hope."

She hated herself for flinching first, but she managed to meet his stare after a few seconds.

"Tonight's not the night," Wyatt proclaimed.

"What? Why the fuck not?" She jerked, shoving herself against him enough to strain the proof of her innocence and cause another jolt to shock her system. "Haven't I waited long enough? What's wrong with me now?"

Wyatt retreated, leaving her empty and bereft. "Jesus, Hope. There's nothing the matter with you. Don't you get it? You deserve better."

"What did I tell you about men making my choices for me?" Childish or not, she kicked out, catching him in the shin with her heel. "If you won't do it, get the hell away. Let me out of here."

Before she could bolt, Clayton smothered her protests. He settled over her like a security blanket, snuffing out the flames of her righteous anger. "Sweetheart, you're even lovelier when you're pissed."

He disarmed her by kissing the tip of her nose. "No one's saying we wouldn't like to have you. Tonight or any other. It would be an honor. One of the greatest pleasures of our lives, I'm sure. Something like that is a responsibility too."

When she attempted to object, he silenced her with a kiss. This time the exchange held a bittersweet edge. Careful tenderness tempered his aggressive lust. She hated it. Because she knew some dumb sliver of tissue between her legs had altered the way he saw her.

"When I think of what might have happened Monday..." Wyatt's face had turned nearly purple.

"Stay with us, Wy. That's done and over. But Hope, your initial run at lovemaking isn't going to involve getting fucked fast and furious in the dirt." Clayton agreed with his partner. "This time I'm going to have to side with Wyatt. You deserve way better than that. Candles and romance. Silk sheets. Permanence."

"All I want is you. And you." She pointed to each of them in turn.

"You'll regret—"

"I *know* you're not telling me what I'll feel, right? I'm woman enough to make up my own mind. This is what I've chosen. How dare you tell me I don't know myself after twenty-three years as well as you do after a few days?" She challenged either of them to argue.

Wyatt sat on his haunches. The pose did nothing to hide his still raging erection. Clayton's similar state was obvious given the thick shaft resting heavy on her abdomen. "Clayton, fix this. You're the talker."

"I think this might be a situation better served by doing." He smiled sadly.

Hope smelled victory.

Until she realized there were a lot of ways to fulfill his prophecy that didn't involve penetration. Clay slithered down her body, pressing a trail of open-mouthed kisses to every bit of her he could reach. He worshipped her figure and stole her ability to debate.

There were worse things than letting him resume the impressive exercise he'd engaged in earlier. One last time, she opened her mouth, but Wyatt anticipated her and thwarted her objection by sinking over her on his knees. One pressed into the blanket on either side of her head. Suddenly, her entire world was made up of his heavy balls, his thick shaft and the plump head leaking pre-come between her breasts.

Before he could make a request, she reached up and returned him to her fist. Except this time she didn't release him when she reached the top of his cock. Hope pulled him toward her by the dick, grateful he didn't make her fight to taste him as thoroughly as Clay relished her.

Wyatt slipped between her lips. He painted his arousal across her tongue, feeding her the first real taste of man she'd had. Greedy, she sucked him in an attempt to coax more of the addicting flavor from him. Instead of the porn-worthy BJ she envisioned, she choked. The awkward angle drove him into the roof of her mouth then onward toward her throat.

"Slow down." He lifted up a tad until she couldn't take him all even if she strained her neck. "There's no hurry. As much as I think I should, I'm not leaving and neither is Clayton. Not until we take care of you."

Clay lifted his head long enough to observe her coarse motions, driven more by desire than any sort of finesse. "Wy, it's not that."

"What?" The big man she held in her mouth seemed dazed.

"I think she's new to this too." Clay rubbed her legs, telling her with his caresses that it was okay. "Help her. Teach her, like you taught me."

"Is he right?" Wyatt went hard all over as his muscles constricted. "She's so brave. A natural. Is that true, Hope?"

She nodded, loving the groan he surrendered when her lips and teeth knocked the top and bottom of his extra-firm cock. As implausible as she'd imagined it, he had gotten harder since she first put her hands on him.

"Help me coach her, Clay." He slowly tipped onto his side, counting on his partner to rotate Hope in sync. Wyatt reached for his lover and Clay went willingly into Wy's arms, angling his body so that they formed an equilateral triangle, each of them on their sides, mouth to cock or pussy.

Hope tightened the connection between her and Wyatt, not waiting for instruction to do what came naturally. She drew on him, traced the veiny ridges of his shaft and rubbed the flat of her tongue over the bulbous head of his cock.

Clay continued to rile her, this time burying his face in her saturated folds. He too tucked nearer. He bit her gently when Wyatt lunged, drawing Clay's hips to him and swallowing his friend's cock whole in one long draw.

"Wy." Clayton lifted his mouth long enough to curse. "Don't teach her bad habits. Not at first. Let her enjoy this time."

Wyatt freed Clay long enough to agree. "Take your mouth off me just a second, Hope. Trust me, I want you right there as much as you want to be there."

"Watch him." Clayton instructed before returning his full attention to driving her insane. How did he expect her to concentrate when he did that swirly thing with his tongue combined with the spiraling thing with his fingertip at her entrance?

She rested her head on Wyatt's thigh, observing as he took a firm hold on Clayton's cock. Wy hadn't lied, Clayton was longer. They both were amazingly beautiful creatures. Her heart tripped knowing they held her between them. That they cared enough to make tonight good for her—a memory to last a lifetime.

Unconsciously, she tasted Wyatt again.

"In a minute, Hope." Wyatt smiled at her. "Like this."

He surprised her with his capacity for gentle loving. Opening his mouth, he first kissed the head of Clay's cock. The erotic vision would never leave her mind. His square jaw and Clayton's erection parting those lush, usually serious lips. Unforgettable.

Slowly—so very, very slowly—he drew the easygoing man into his mouth. Along the way he stopped to tease and torture with brushes of his tongue and soft sucks. He backtracked a bit every now and again before taking more.

Clayton increased the pressure of his mouth and hands. She tried to suppress the riot of ecstasy he granted, but when Wyatt's lips finally rested on the slab of muscle at the base of Clay's cock, she lost what little control she had.

Her body betrayed her and flew apart.

Hope screamed their names, asking for mercy or more, she didn't know. She scratched Wyatt's ass as she tried to get closer to him and her heels drummed on the floor of the barn. Horses shuffled nervously next door. None of it mattered. There was nothing she could do but soar on the currents of delight and relief they'd generated within her.

When she could finally see straight again, she struggled to catch her breath. Yet, instead of ending the party early, as she feared, her orgasm had Clayton kissing her sensitive flesh even as he cooed reassurance and praise. Wyatt did the same from where he'd finished his lesson and watched the annihilation of her boundaries instead.

"Can we do that again?" she asked, her pants making her sentences choppy. "Maybe tomorrow. Or the next day. Or every day."

"How about right now?" Clay grinned before dipping down once more.

"Oh my God," she shouted at the surplus of sensation. Wyatt was smart to keep his cock out of her mouth while she adapted to the deluge of rapture they instilled in her.

"Relax, Hope." Wyatt reached toward her and she met him halfway, holding his good hand. "You're beautiful when you come. If you concentrate, he'll help you get there again. Soon. A dozen times, if you want."

"I'll have a heart attack before then," she swore. "I want to do it to you."

"No worries there, sweetheart." Clay interrupted his pattern. "I nearly shot all over Wyatt's face when you flooded my mouth. Do it again and I'm likely to lose it. And usually that's enough to set Wyatt off too. With your pink lips surrounding him, he won't stand a chance."

She didn't hesitate to practice the lesson Wyatt had provided.

If the happy gurgle he made was any indication, she figured she was doing something right. The thrust of his hips in a repetitive arc that matched the one she made across Clay's face served as the final bit of evidence she needed to intensify her efforts.

Soon it wasn't just her vocalizing the heady, addictive, amazing impact they were having on her nervous system. All three of them seemed to crest in unison, servicing one of their trio while accepting similar treatment from another. Linked, they shared in the experience.

Hope never wanted their session to end. She shouldn't have been so hasty in dismissing the dozen climaxes they'd promised. Except she knew it wouldn't be quite so appetizing without them flying right alongside her.

She moaned and Wyatt bulged in her mouth. Clay grunted against her pussy, sending shockwaves of desire through her genitals. Never had she craved something more than she wanted to come with them at that moment. Sharing this with them meant everything to her.

They got her and she got them. They were meant to fit together like this. She *knew*. She hadn't been wrong. This could never be anything but absolutely right.

"Wyatt!" Her warning would have been completely unintelligible if they weren't so in tune with her and she with them. He groaned and Clayton grunted. They were there, on the edge with her. For once, she wasn't alone.

The pure bliss that percolated through every cell of her being with that knowledge set her off with the force of a meteor strike. She imploded beneath the release of energy that threatened to have them all going up in a mushroom cloud. At the pinnacle of her trajectory through rapture, cream poured from Wyatt's cock, coating the roof of her mouth and encouraging her to suck him dry.

At the same time, Clayton first froze, then went wild, coaxing her into another mini-peak while he unleashed his own come down Wyatt's throat.

Hope swallowed reflexively, drinking all Wyatt gave her even as he and Clay did the same for their counterparts. Together they melted into an interlinked blob of satisfied customers.

Someone jostled her from her sated trance when they flipped around. Clayton. He cuddled up to her back and kept the chill from reaching her now that perspiration cooled on her skin. Wyatt didn't miss out. He joined them, facing his two lovers as he snuggled to her from head to toe. The weight of her breasts felt full and heavy where they pressed against his chest.

The guys draped their arms over her and the man beyond until they were laced into an unbreakable knot of limbs.

"You did great." Wyatt kissed her long and slow before tipping her chin toward Clayton.

"So fearless. So talented. It took me a few tries before I could make him shoot that fast." Clay winked at her. "You really must be top of your class, huh?"

"If I were the professor, you'd have aced my exam." Wyatt grinned, then yawned.

"I can't believe you did that after how sick you were yesterday." She checked his face for signs of strain and found none, though his lids did droop.

"You're the best medicine a guy could ask for." He tried to smother another yawn, but neither she nor Clayton were about to let him off the hook. As amazing as this felt, she wouldn't risk his health.

Before they could call the game, she extricated herself from their grasp and rooted around for her dress. Flashing her ass at them earned her a swat. She enjoyed the sting enough to do it again.

"Will you take me home?" She nibbled her lip, wondering if they'd mind Daniel and her cousins seeing them with her. "You could leave me at the end of the lane if you'd rather. But I have an assignment to do and class almost as early as you two have to be back here. Wyatt can't skimp on sleep either."

She stared at Clayton and he nodded.

"You're right. It's time to go home." He got to his feet, yanking her close before tugging on his jeans. The kiss he laid on her lips was fierce and thorough. "But we're not letting you traipse around in the dark. Are we, Wy?"

The other man didn't seem as certain. After all, he'd sworn her to secrecy, hadn't he?

"No, we're not." As if her safety wouldn't win out above all else with him. "Let's go. We're lucky no one came looking for her in here."

"You can thank Sterling later, I'm sure." Hope smiled as the two cowboys shimmied into their jeans, which fit like second skin. "She likes snooty red wine."

"Good to know." Clay plucked a blade of hay from her hair. "Maybe Friday we could have you over for dinner, and you could tell us more about what *you* like?"

Hope glanced at Wyatt. He nodded slowly.

"I'd love to join you. But let's not tempt fate. I'll do the cooking." She darted out of the stall and toward their truck when they attempted to spank her. They gave chase, but let her win the race. No way would their long legs have trouble catching up...

Unless they were as uncoordinated as she felt in the aftermath of their loving.

"So how was your first time?" Sterling perched on the edge of Hope's bed and played with her hair, finger combing out the knots. Her adventurous cousin had gotten home late. Third time this week. Maybe she was seeing someone too?

"Ask me in twenty years. Maybe I'll have lost my virginity by then." She pounded her fist on the down pillow she had tried desperately to fall asleep on for the past two hours, to no avail.

"Oh, Hope." Her cousin unclenched the fingers trembling in her hold as she rescued the poor bedding from further abuse. "What happened? I thought for sure..."

"They realized I had no experience pretty quick. Up until then it was great, and the stuff after, I wouldn't turn it down if they offered to do it again." She sighed. "But full-out sex, they wouldn't. Not tonight. Not in the barn. Maybe never."

"Damn men with a sense of chivalry. Didn't that bullshit die out a century ago?" Sterling knew just how to cheer her up. "Recreational sex between consenting adults is one of the few perks to being a grown up. It's not all I'd imagined as a kid. Work. Bills. Worrying about our family and friends. Life is...a lot. Sex is the best anxiety reliever I know of. Can't they just toss you a bang and move on?"

"I know, right?" Hope didn't dare admit, maybe even to herself, that she had her sights set on a hell of a lot more than a physical exchange. As badly as her body wanted to revolt right now, Wy and Clay had endeared themselves to her even more with their show of tenderness and caution. Damn them.

They'd cared for her and refused to disrespect her, at least in their understanding of the world. She couldn't truly fault them for that, could she?

"I'm done with chasing them, Sterling." She sighed as she melted into her comfortable bed, less on edge once her mind was made up. "If they want traditional mixed with their ménage, then they're going to have to come for me."

"Oh, make them grovel." Sterling tucked in beside Hope, sensing she didn't relish the thought of being alone. "Maybe even insist on some wooing."

"What the hell does that even mean?" Hope laughed as she smacked her cousin with her pillow.

"I don't know. It's something Vivi says. Like 'courting'. Or 'going steady'." Sterling sighed. "It sounds kind of romantic. Old fashioned and simpler than the world we live in."

Hope didn't have it in her to ask about the source of Sterling's disgruntlement. She would save that discussion for another time, when she could lend her full attention and support. Tonight, they both seemed content to let it drop while they each dreamed about what would make them happiest.

"Good night, Hope."

"Night, Sterling. I'm so glad the Compass Girls are all girls."

"Dumbass." Sterling giggled, a sound rare for the more mature member of their group. "Go to sleep."

They both drifted off with smiles on their faces.

Chapter Eight

A few days later, Hope carried a chocolate raspberry cake up to the main house while her cousins trailed with balloons, a card and the present they'd gone in on together for Vivi. It was the big seven-one for their grandmother. They'd all tried to avoid mentioning how cruel it was that despite rising average life expectancies, Vivi wouldn't see the top end of that scale. Or at least she wouldn't remember it.

They'd made a fuss, knowing they only had so many of these opportunities left.

Sienna raced ahead to open the door. Her brows knitted together when she found it locked. They never were barred from the main house. "What the heck?"

Hope glanced over her shoulder. "Her car isn't here."

"Where would she have gone?" Jade didn't usually freak about minor stuff, but her voice rose a full octave when she wondered aloud.

"Get the key." Sterling lifted her chin toward the hanging flowerpot that housed the spare. Everyone and their brother knew it was there and had been for decades. One reason no one ever bothered to lock the door.

Sienna did the honors, then helped them all in. They set their goodies on the kitchen table and flipped on a light. The countertop separating the kitchen from the living room housed a gorgeous bouquet.

"Maybe she went out to an early dinner with whoever brought her those?" Hope suggested.

"Let's see." Sienna crossed the space as familiar to them as their own homes. She plucked the card from a riot of roses and wildflowers that made an eclectic centerpiece—classic, romantic and a little untamed.

When she gasped and pressed her hand over her heart, including the card, the rest of the cousins crept closer. Hope asked, "What's wrong, See?"

"Who are they from?" Sterling narrowed her eyes.

"It says, 'Eternally in love with you, JD.'" A tear trickled down Sienna's pretty face as she recited the heartbreaking message.

"Who would prank her like this? And where the hell did she go?" Jade's fists made it clear she'd like to pummel the asshole who'd done this to their grandmother. Whether they'd had good intentions or not, they'd obviously affected her. Everyone knew Vivi was as madly in love with her long-lost husband as she had been the day they'd gotten married.

Toying with her feelings didn't endear anyone to her grandkids. Especially not when they understood how delicate a balance Vivi was maintaining right now. She'd mostly stopped driving on her own and usually preferred to take one of the Compass Girls with her when she ventured out. Stress made her memory lapses more frequent and pronounced.

"I wonder how long she's been gone." Hope checked around. The coffee pot had an inch of dark liquid in it. Stone cold, it held no warmth when she pressed her fingers to the appliance. Breakfast dishes sat in the sink.

"Seems like a while. She didn't even leave a light on and it'll be dark in an hour or so." Sienna looked from cousin to cousin.

"I'm calling the florist." Jade snatched the card from the counter and slipped her cell from her pocket. She waved the phone near the paper and the embedded chip plugged the number into the phone before confirming her cousin wanted to connect to the small business.

Jade flipped the phone to speaker. All four of them held their breath until Nancy Plack picked up. "April Showers, Nancy speaking. How may I help you?"

"Hi, this is Jade Compton. I'm calling because I'm wondering who paid to send flowers to my grandmother this morning? I realize they probably thought they were doing a good deed, but Vivi is still grieving—"

"Jade, hang on." The woman they'd gone to school with had started training to take over her parents' business. A friend, she wouldn't lie to them. "I know it's kind of odd... But your grandfather sent those flowers. My dad told me that when JD first found out he had cancer, he came in the store and arranged for a prime bouquet to be sent to Mrs. Compton every year on her birthday. He tried to pay an arm and a leg. My parents were so touched, they donated his money to the memorial scholarship fund set up in his name at the college."

"Oh." Even Jade had nothing to say to that.

Hope wiped tears from her cheeks with the back of her hands as Sienna and Sterling sniffed openly. What would it be like to find a man to love her like that? Endlessly. Stumbling on a true soul mate seemed like a one in a million chance. Never mind discovering two in a lifetime.

Her family had been lucky in love. Even Sienna had Daniel now. Maybe she'd taken their streak for granted. What if she broke the trend?

"Besides, no offense, but my mom says JD's funeral singlehandedly kept our business thriving for a decade. We owe your family a lot. The flowers are the least we could do. Did she enjoy them?" Nancy sounded so pleased with her work, which was admittedly gorgeous, that none of the Compass Girls had the heart to tell the woman what they suspected.

"They're lovely, Nancy. Thank you." Jade cleared her throat.

"You're welcome. Sorry, Jade, but there's a line forming in here..."

"Go on, make people happy." She swallowed hard, all of them knowing somehow JD's surprise hadn't worked this year. "We'll see you soon, maybe have a girl's night out."

"Sounds like fun. Tell your grandmother happy birthday from us."

"You got it. Bye." Jade somehow managed to hang up before a sob caught in her throat.

The Compass Girls rushed together, linking arms in a group hug.

"Damn men," Sterling growled. "They're always causing problems."

"Only because we love them too much." Sienna sighed, no doubt thinking of her wounded cowboy. Daniel had well and truly lassoed her heart.

Hope didn't speak, but she thought back to Wyatt's face last night when he'd realized she was a virgin. His tenderness when he'd refused to give her less than she deserved made it impossible to stay angry at him for leaving her hanging. And he hadn't, really.

Same for Clay, who'd given her more pleasure with his mouth and hands alone than she'd imagined could come from full penetration. In reality, the connection between them had shaded everything they'd done together. The individual acts mattered less than the general emotion they inspired.

She couldn't imagine the mortal wound it would cause to have that bond grow and strengthen for years, through most of a lifetime, only to have it yanked away. How had Vivi survived? Sure, she had her family, but maybe there were days—like today—where that just wasn't enough.

"We have to find her." Jade came to her senses first. "The sun is setting and the nights are still chilly. You know how she gets cold quickly these days. Why the hell didn't we buy her a matching cell phone before now?"

They all glared at their brightly wrapped gift. It had been a precaution they agreed Vivi needed these days. If they'd thought of it sooner, they could simply call their grandmother. Assuming she wouldn't have forgotten the damn thing in the house.

"We need to do some damage control, girls." Sterling took the reins. "I'll call the Mothers and tell them we're going to take Vivi to a birthday dinner. Hope and See, you guys go round up Daniel and whoever else will keep their mouth shut from the barn. Jade, head over to Liam's spread. Maybe he's seen her and, if not, he can help us look."

She stared at Hope.

As much as she hated begging for favors, especially from Wyatt and Clayton, she knew the guys would pitch in if she asked.

"We'll divide and conquer. Thank God Compton Pass isn't very big." Sterling already had her phone to her ear and spoke the voice command to dial her mom.

"Come on." Sienna snagged Hope's elbow and dragged her toward the barn. "Put on your big girl panties. It's for Vivi."

Hope didn't answer. She was too busy thinking of how to ask for help when she'd wanted nothing more than to put some distance between her and the guys who'd set her on fire, to see if they'd felt the heat too. Playing games wasn't usually her style. Pride dictated her ultimatum this time though. Tired of fishing, she prepared to don a stony mask. Again.

"Damn it." She kicked a rock against the barn door before heading inside.

Sienna stared at her. "You cursed."

"Seems like it's getting to be a habit with your cousin. She's got a dirty mouth." Of course. Wy had to be right fucking there, didn't he? On the other side of the barn door, Daniel, Wyatt and Clayton were shooting the shit as they wrapped up their day. The bosses had all gone home early to spruce up for Vivi's family party this evening.

"You didn't seem to have any complaints about my mouth yesterday." She didn't give a shit if Daniel's eyes got as big as one of the horses in the stall nearby.

Wyatt was saved from answering when Sienna threw herself against Daniel's chest. As if a dam broke, she sobbed, clinging to his shoulders.

"What the—?" He rubbed her back and held her close even as he looked to Hope for answers.

"It's Vivi. She's missing." A lump formed in her own throat.

"Oh, shit." Daniel looked to Wyatt and Clayton. Of course he knew about the disease slowly stealing their grandmother, but he'd been conditioned to keep the Compass Girls' secret.

"What aren't you saying?" Clayton approached. She flinched when he reached out. His gentle touch would only reduce her to bawling that matched Sienna's. No one needed that.

Sterling's directive echoed in Hope's mind. Round up whoever will keep their mouth shut.

"You can't tell anyone what I'm about to share." Hope crossed her arms to keep from reaching for one or both of the men who nodded solemnly. "My grandmother has Alzheimer's disease. It's getting worse. You saw it yourself last night when she called you the wrong names. She's slipping more and more. Her doctor enrolled her in clinical trials since she has an aggressive type, but she's not responding as well to the formula as they'd hoped. Unfortunately, they can't hide much from me. I can sense their disappointment."

Sienna choked up again, burying her face in Daniel's neck while he crooned softly to her.

"Hell, Hope. I'm sorry." Wyatt bundled her beneath his good arm and yanked her to his side before she could object. "Your family is keeping this damn quiet."

"They don't know." She trembled, grateful when he hugged her tighter. "Only the Compass Girls—and Daniel, and now you guys—do."

"That's a heavy load to dump on you." Clayton touched her cheek softly, mindful of the lightening bruise there.

"Thank you," Daniel scoffed. "I don't think she realizes how much she's imposing on them."

"We can debate that another time." Hope ignored the dread lining her stomach at the idea of her parents finding out about her lie of omission. They'd be disappointed in her. "Right now, I was wondering…"

"Of course we'll search with you." Wyatt didn't let her finish. "Clay will have to drive, but I'm coming along."

"I'll take Sienna in my truck and head to town. You three check north from here. Jade can pick up Liam, then go south, while Sterling stays here in case she returns." Daniel directed on the move. They dashed toward their vehicles, meeting the other two Compass Girls in the yard.

"South, got it." Jade nodded as she hopped on the back of her motorcycle. She tore out of the lot first, flinging gravel before launching down the lane that led to the main road and Liam's place.

Clayton grabbed the keys Wyatt tossed him from mid-air, then followed suit. Wyatt opened the door, which squeaked on slightly rusted hinges. She grabbed the handle on top of the door then hoisted herself. With his good hand, Wyatt boosted her. His big palm cupped her ass perfectly.

She glared at him as he joined her on the bench seat.

"What?" His smirk tempted her to lick it. "Just trying to be helpful."

Clay chuckled as he started the engine with a roar and set them off behind the other two vehicles. Dust swirled around them. The resulting artificial fog lent the evening an ominous edge.

Hope shivered.

Wyatt slung his arm around her shoulders and tucked her against the trunk of his body again. Heat rolled off him as if he were a living furnace. She murmured, "Do you still have a fever?"

"No." He shook his head. "The doc cleared me for light duty today."

"He's always warm." Clay's deepening tone made Hope shift in Wyatt's hold. She remembered that sound from Sunday night.

Rural roads flew by on their left and right. They drove faster than wise, though not too quick to keep them from examining the ditches for Vivi's little red sedan. So far, no luck. Hope swept her gaze from side to side, not wanting to miss an inch of the landscape. Besides, keeping busy meant she didn't focus on the pressure of Wyatt's thigh on hers or the skill with which Clay handled the truck. Just like he'd done with her.

On the border of Clarke, the town adjoining Compton Pass, they passed a turn off to the Wilsons' farm. It'd been abandoned for nearly five years now. With advancements in farming, less land was needed to produce the same yield. Plus, too many people had stuck to old ways of doing things. Modern farms, or those that ran most efficiently, had survived. Others had not been so lucky.

Hope figured Uncle Sam and Uncle Seth were smart to have proposed expanding the Compton name to horse breeding. Another egg in the basket acted as insurance. More diversity in their businesses meant they'd be less likely to go the way of some of the legacy operations. They'd been grandiose in their time.

Heck, Vivi had told them often about the Wilsons' parties...

"Wait!" Hope clenched Clay's knee so hard he slammed on the brakes, skidding to a stop on the side of the road. "Turn the truck around. I know a place she might have gone."

Without questioning her instincts, he three-pointed it right there and did as she asked.

"Where am I going?" His stare tracked the winding center line as if glued to it.

"Take the next left." She pointed. "Slow down. This hasn't been used for a while. Except maybe by local kids as a make-out spot."

"You ever come out here with a boy?" Wyatt surprised her with his curiosity.

"Don't worry about that." She couldn't get tangled in their game of want-you-but-don't-want-you right now. It confused her heart and mind even when she wasn't distracted.

"Maybe we'll bring you back another time." Wyatt tucked her hair behind her ear.

"He's trying to take your mind off your grandmother." Clayton spared her a quick smile. "It tears him up when someone he cares about is upset. Just another kind of hurt, Hope."

"I'll be okay as soon as we..." Up ahead, a flash of red caught her attention through the newly budding foliage. "Vivi!"

The instant Clay swung to a stop, the truck at an odd angle in their haste, she nearly climbed over Wyatt to launch herself from the cab.

"Hope, wait." He winced as he grabbed her windbreaker with his still-healing fingers. "We're going with you."

He slowed her enough that Clayton joined them. Each man took one of her hands as they sprinted for the barn. A trail of footprints squished the spring grass shoots into the slightly muddy earth. They led from Vivi's car to the half-collapsed barn nearby.

"Vivi," Hope called out, not wanting to startle the woman.

It wasn't an answer that returned. A scratchy ballad curled through the mossy trees instead.

Hope lurched to a stop on the perimeter of the dilapidated structure. Through a hole in the wall, she spotted her grandmother—arms up, dancing with the brisk air as she sang and laughed. Her steps were light and fluid, her eyes alive in a way Hope hadn't realized she'd never seen from the brilliant woman before.

"Where is she?" Clay whispered to Hope. "*When* is she?"

"So long ago." Hope whimpered. "This is where she met my grandfather, JD. At a party. She told me once that she knew the moment she met him that they were meant to be together."

"Ah, damn." Wyatt bent over, bracing his hands on his knees. "She looks so happy."

"In love." She swallowed hard. That starry-eyed gaze—she'd caught it creeping onto her own face lately as she stepped from the shower with thoughts of these two men front and center in her mind.

"How can you survive without someone that's a part of you?" He looked up at Clayton, fear rampant in his gaze. "Pretty stupid to take that chance."

"I bet if you asked her, she wouldn't trade a second of what they shared. Even if it didn't last as long as they'd planned." Clay was quick to counter Wy's arguments, though he didn't point out the obvious. Whether he admitted it to himself or not, Wyatt had already made that leap of faith with Clay.

Hope could see both sides. Watching her grandmother twirl, she knew she would be the one to return the woman to a world that didn't include the man of her dreams.

"I can go get her," Clay offered as if he could sense her dread.

"No. She won't know you. I don't want to scare her." A deep breath or two later, she steeled herself for what was to come. As she took a tiny step forward, then another, she heard Wyatt mumbling in the background.

"Daniel, we have her. Meet us at the old Wilson place in Clarke. Hope's going to need her cousins." The man proved her fathers had chosen wisely in making him a team lead on the ranch. He understood people as well as he did animals. His natural social intelligence made it tougher to dismiss his concerns about the future, about her ability to cope with sex devoid of emotion.

Damn him. More to consider. Later.

"Vivi." Hope tried again to reach through time. "It's getting late, dark. Would you like to go home?"

Vicki Compton turned toward her. Even the voice she spoke in bore little resemblance to the woman Hope called Vivi. "Hello! Nice to meet you. Gatherings around here only get started at dusk. After the ranching day is done. Going home now would be silly."

Hope relegated her tears to a place deep inside. She could unleash them once this nightmare had ended. Guilt lashed her for what she was about to do. "I'm sorry, Vivi. You're not at a party yet. It *is* your birthday, though. You're seventy-one years old today."

"You have such an imagination." Vivi laughed. "Let me introduce you to my new friend, JD. He'll love your stories. What's your name?"

"Hope. Hope Compton. I'm your granddaughter, Vivi." She wrung her hands as an initial flicker of awareness splintered the elderly woman's fantasy.

Shaking her head, she squinted, as if trying to see an oasis once the edges of a mirage had started to become apparent. Confusion set in. "Lucy? Is that Silas and Colby over there?"

"No, Vivi." She swallowed hard before trying again. "I'm Hope. Lucy's daughter. Those cowboys are Wyatt and Clayton. Remember, they came to dinner last night? At your house. On Compass Ranch."

Vivi nearly ripped Hope's heart out when she looked up at the rotting rafters and asked, "Where did the lights go? The garland of wildflowers?"

Neither Hope nor Vivi could constrain their anguish when her grandmother whispered, "JD."

She crumpled to the floor.

Hope held her grandmother as the woman grieved all over again for her lost husband. The Compass Girls had witnessed this misery before. Every time Vivi forgot he was gone then remembered was like a million razors slashing her soul into shreds.

Hope sometimes wondered if Vivi would be happier ignorant. Peaceful without knowledge of her unintended autonomy.

"My love. He's gone, isn't he?" Her breathing hitched as spasms jerked her shoulders in Hope's light grasp.

"I'm sorry, Vivi." It was all Hope could keep saying. "I'm so sorry."

Beams of light roved across Hope and the woman she adored. Shortly after, the crash of people tearing through the brush made it clear the rest of the Compass Girls were incoming.

"Vivi!"

They shouted for their grandmother as they approached. By the time they entered the structure, Vivi had composed herself more than Hope could have imagined possible. The strongest woman she knew got to her feet on her own and dusted off her knees.

Is this the caliber of acting she'd been doing these past several months?

Hope shuddered as she realized the disease was progressing far more rapidly than they'd feared. She'd have to call Vivi's doctor first thing in the morning.

Maybe it was time to tell the Mothers.

Thank God they wouldn't have to break the news to their fathers alone. The men would be crushed. Losing their dad had altered the course of their lives. But Vivi had held them all together. Who would do that now?

Sienna reached them first. She and Daniel wrapped a blanket around Vivi, whose skin felt chilly to the touch. They hugged her, confessing how worried they'd been. Sterling and Jade followed a few heartbeats behind. They showered Vivi with hugs and relief that reminded them all how fortunate they were to have her while maybe never realizing that their grandmother had suffered devastation beyond imagining.

Hope could honestly say she'd never viscerally comprehended the depth of Vivi's loss like she did after what she'd witnessed minutes ago. As long as she lived, she'd never forget that pain. Is that what Wyatt dealt with too?

JD had been stolen by fate. Guilt over the tragic, untimely loss of an innocent would amplify the despair. Not that Hope thought for one second that the child Wy had also been could have been responsible in any way. But she knew him well enough to guess he would see things differently.

Blinking, she tried to focus on what Vivi said to calm the Compass Girls and the guys supporting them.

"I got those flowers from JD, like every year, and they made me miss him. That's all. I just needed some time to myself to think. I guess I lost track of time." She lied with such grace that the rest of the Compass Girls must have assumed their grandmother's bloodshot eyes were earned from hours of poised, cognizant weeping instead of the crash landing with reality Hope, Wyatt and Clayton had observed.

She stared over at the two men. Neither of them called Vivi out on her exploitation of the truth. How could they, when they'd seen how hard she was fighting to keep things straight? To maintain this illusion for her family?

Wyatt held his arms out, open. Hope ran to him and threw herself against his strong, vital chest. Clayton closed rank, protecting her from the horror of what they'd seen and the sense of impending doom.

Because Vivi wasn't getting better.

There was no going back.

Not even with today's medicine and all the research that had been conducted on this horrible disease. Progress had been made, but not for the specific brand of sickness that attacked Vivi. Not even the clinical trial, their last bastion of optimism, could keep reality at bay any longer.

Time was finite. Every second with her grandmother was precious. Even more than that, every instant of life was too. It could be Hope's turn tomorrow.

She didn't want to waste another second.

Enough lingering in this painful purgatory. She had her sights set on the two men she wanted. And she planned to convince them to take advantage of her.

Tonight.

Chapter Nine

Hope had refused to bail out of Vivi's birthday party. Though she'd considered telling her parents that something she'd eaten at her imaginary dinner with her grandmother and cousins hadn't sat right with her, she could no longer pretend.

This might be the last time she could celebrate with her whole family.

After what they'd seen, Wyatt and Clayton didn't object. They even accepted when she invited them to stay. They seemed to understand the fragility of her happy façade. By her side, they ensured no one had access to shatter her. It was enough that her insides were broken—rattling around, bruising her heart and soul. She was surprised no one could hear the shards clinking together.

After an hour, she couldn't take anymore. If she had to fake another smile her face would crack in half. Even her healing eye ached a bit after days of feeling fine. Slipping into the bathroom, she sat on the lid of the toilet with her head in her hands long enough that two knocks came and went.

Finally one stronger than the others refused to be ignored.

"You okay?" Wyatt asked through the solid wood.

"Yeah, can't a girl pee?" She didn't have the gumption to stand and face him.

He did the work for her. A little rattle later and the doorknob jiggled. "That'd be a world-record piss. What'd you drink? Forty-seven gallons of water this morning? I'm coming in. So if I'm wrong, pull up your panties, assuming you actually bothered to put some on today."

"Get in here and keep your voice quiet." Her hands waved, palms down, as she moved them toward the floor in an attempt to mute his booming bass.

Wyatt sat on the edge of the claw foot tub so he faced her. "What're you hiding from?"

"My parents, mostly." She shrugged. "I hate lying to them. It's not how we do things in our family."

"Must be nice." Wyatt winced. "I didn't mean that in an asshole way. I really meant it must be great to have people you can trust with everything."

She reached out to hold his hands. "You have Clayton."

He nodded. "I don't deserve him yet somehow, yeah, I guess he's mine."

"You could have *me* if you wanted." Too tired to care if she sounded pathetic, she told the truth. "Hell, even if you never fuck me, you can still count on me. Whether you see it or not, you *are* worthy of unconditional love. You're human, Wyatt. That's all it takes. If someone implied otherwise, screw them."

"It turns me on when you swear." He squeezed her fingers, letting her know he hadn't missed her message or taken it for granted.

"In that case... Shit. Damn. Hell."

Wyatt's gaze heated until she wondered if his control would finally melt. He leaned forward as she escalated her swearing. Close enough to kiss.

"Ass. Cock. *Fuck*." She really got into the last one, meeting him in the middle. A hairsbreadth separated her potty mouth from his decadent grin.

"Hope?" Uncle Sam asked from the other side of the door before rapping lightly. "Uh, is everything all right in there?"

She jumped and might have tumbled from her throne if not for Wyatt's steadying grip. She waved him into the shower, then yanked the curtain closed before cracking the door. "Sorry. I'm kind of having a girl problem. Can you send Sterling or Jade or Sienna?"

Nothing would get rid of a pesky man faster than that old fib. "Yeah, sure. Right away."

He'd already retreated down the hall.

"What happened to your no-lying policy?" Wyatt stepped out, laughing at her in the mirror.

"I didn't. Guys are the biggest trouble a woman could have." She shook her head.

When Jade poked her head in, she got the gist. "I'll make sure the coast is clear. I recommend leaving one at a time, a few minutes apart."

"Good plan." Wyatt nodded. "Rendezvous at my truck. We're getting out of here."

"I like the way you think." Hope blew him a kiss before strutting from the bathroom, finally feeling as if something might be going her way.

Clayton couldn't stop glancing at the two people lounging in his living room. They'd piled on to the ugly couch, then dug into the smuggled ice cream from Vivi's party, taking turns licking vanilla and sprinkles from a bent serving spoon. None of them really gave a shit about the sappy movie playing out on their tiny projector screen.

At least the drama gave him a good reason to hold Hope. She didn't resist when he put his arms around her and tilted her onto the plane of his chest. Wyatt continued the chain by doing the same to Clay. He could empathize with the unflagging erection jabbing his lower back. Certain Hope required comfort—not sweaty sex—Clay buried his hunger, staring at the movie while his mind wandered.

Instead of the actress spilling crocodile tears, all he could see was the way Hope had looked as she'd rescued her grandmother from a quagmire of memories.

Heartbroken.

Part of the girl he and Wyatt had fallen so hard for in the past two weeks had disappeared forever, right in front of his eyes. Destroyed. Harsh reality had stolen some of her innocence—the kind of guilelessness that originated from the protection of her family's empire rather than a simple biological barrier. It was like Two Lefts all over again.

It made him long to give her something amazing to replace her lost confidence in humanity. Proof that the world didn't always suck and not all her adult discoveries had to be negative ones. Wyatt seemed pensive, even more so than usual. Was he considering a demonstration too? Or tallying all the dumb reasons he had to be afraid of what they both craved?

"I want Hope to spend the night," Clay blurted. No reason he and Wy had to pre-discuss every damn step they took with their girl. Maybe if the odds were in his favor—Hope's and his passion versus Wy's logic—he might have more success.

"I'd like that too." She nuzzled deeper into his hold, causing him to dream of all sorts of ways to pass the hours until dawn.

"Sure, okay." Wyatt shrugged, raising and lowering them in his hold.

"Does anyone care about how this flick winds up?" Clay reached for the remote.

"I've actually seen it before," Hope admitted. "It's not that great. I hate sad endings."

"Time for bed, Wyatt." He shifted until the three of them rose from the couch together. "Let's snuggle right. Our bed may not be enormous, but at least I won't have a spring jammed up my ass."

"I thought you liked that." Wyatt ruffled his hair.

"I'm not sure I remember." Clayton shoved his roommate as they crossed into their private space and tumbled onto the mattress covered in utilitarian sheets with a blue gingham print. Patting the space between them, he encouraged Hope to take the middle position. Dressed only in one of his faded tractor supply T-shirts, she looked more beautiful than anyone had a right to as she crawled into the place of honor. "It's been forever since we had sex. I'm starting to think you planned to dump me along with Boone."

Though he laughed as he said it, neither of his bedmates was fooled.

Hope knotted their fingers and held tight while Wyatt swallowed hard and stared at his big feet, which poked out from beneath the bottom edge of the covers. "I'm sorry, Clay. I feel like I let you down. I know you liked him."

"It would never have worked. You were right. We're both into women. It might have taken me longer to crack, but I would have, and he only would have been hurt more down the road. Thank you for suffering the heat for me. I know you did it on purpose." Relief allowed him to take a deep breath for the first time in months. Why had that been so damn hard to say without Hope holding his hand?

Insulation. Glue. She was both.

"Maybe the lion has a heart after all?" Hope stared at Wyatt with so much admiration and pride that it touched Clayton. To see someone else value the man he held in such high regard made him appreciate her twice as much. Not everyone could look past Wy's gruff exterior. She had from the very first moment.

"If I had one of those, I wouldn't be considering putting on a show for you right now, even knowing how you'll take it. That it'll raise the stakes in your romantic mind for something that simply can't happen. How valiant is that?" He groaned. "Don't tell me I didn't warn you when the fun is over."

Plllbt! Hope blew him a full-on, cheek flapping, tongue wagging raspberry.

It took a hell of a lot to catch the tough guy off guard. Clayton reveled in the wide-eyed shock on his boyfriend's handsome face at the outrageous gesture.

"Did you just fucking *plllbt* me?" Wyatt looked like he might take Hope over his knee after he mimicked her juvenile display, which somehow managed to convey her feelings precisely.

When had Wyatt last looked so young? So carefree? Hell, he was twenty-seven going on fifty most of the time. A hint of the kid he'd been before his sister's accident rose to the surface.

Clay cracked up at their antics, though he knew they weren't entirely joking around. He hadn't found something that called to him as much as their playfulness since the first time he rode a horse. The freedom, the control, the perfect partnership of man and animal—or best friends… "Oh God, I love you two."

He didn't realize he'd uttered his informal declaration until they both whipped around to stare at him. Wyatt sputtered.

"I mean. You know. Uh. Well, just calm down a minute. I meant the little-l kind of love." *Sure you did, buddy.*

Wyatt rolled his eyes and set them all laughing again. Disaster averted.

Climbing to her knees between them, Hope's eyes twinkled. She snaked one of her hands onto each of them. "Will you show me what it's like between you?"

Generosity and kindness shaped her soft smile as she peeked at him.

"It's okay, Hope. I'd rather take care of you." When Clay reached for her, she swayed out of his grasp.

"I'm curious. And, um, kind of embarrassed that I don't know more. What better way to learn what each of you likes than to see you get it on? You've had an awful lot of practice, I assume?" Her tongue snuck out, wetting the spot where her plump lip had split so recently. The reminder of her ex-boyfriend and how he'd dismissed her requests made Clay eager to comply.

"We've done each other once or twice." He shrugged and glanced at the bulge in Wyatt's pajama pants. The soft cotton did nothing to disguise the rampant hard-on threatening the drawstring waist.

It'd been forever since he'd been filled. Held and loved through action, if not words. He'd buried the need to hear what he knew to be true.

Wyatt shifted so that his arm blocked their line of sight.

"You'd say no to that?" Hope raised a brow at Wyatt before shifting her gaze back to Clayton. The raw esteem in her pretty almond eyes pumped him full of smugness and confidence.

Pour on the heat, why not? It took a hell of a lot to crack Wyatt's control, true. Yet today had taxed them all. The smoldering connections between them, the misery and panic of Vivi's disappearance, the realization that all of them were subject to life's ticking clock—those things shoved them toward the brink.

He grabbed the hem of his white tank and raised it, bit by bit, until the arrowhead Wyatt had given him nearly twenty years ago came into view. Clay never took it off. Not even to shower. Wyatt had told him the thing had existed for hundreds of years. Like their friendship would.

Clay had carried his best friend's promise in his back pocket for nearly a decade until Wyatt had surprised him one Christmas by turning it into a necklace. He'd never admitted it, but he'd sobbed when he'd presumed the token lost. Having it returned to him, enhanced, had been one of the best moments of his life. A gift he would never forget or take for granted.

Could Hope be another talisman? Bringing Wyatt back to him after their disastrous affair with Boone? Maybe enhancing what they'd had before, though the concept seemed surreal.

"I don't have a lot of willpower when it comes to this man." Wyatt shook his head. "I can never say no for long."

"It feels like forever," Clay whispered.

As if he were a snake lying in the meadow—coiled yet motionless—Wyatt sprang to action, striking before Clay could react. Wy barreled into him, knocking him from his side to his back, covering him completely. Damn, Clay had missed this.

"He practically drools when I pin his arms over his head." Wyatt glanced at Hope. The flicker made it clear he intended to put on a hell of a performance for their filly. Maybe he thought he could shoo her with his intensity. Clay knew that was a pointless endeavor. But he didn't mind letting Wyatt herd him. Enjoying the hell out of the experience would be more like it.

Too bad he'd left his bullwhip and riding crops out in the barn.

Eh, maybe they should ease Hope into that.

Before he could spend much more time debating the merits of Wyatt's expert leather handling, the man returned his focus to the here and now by grinding his hard cock over Clay's. The feel of their shafts rubbing together through their thin pants had him gritting his teeth on a groan.

No shame. No inhibitions. No dignity.

When Wyatt claimed his mate, Clay surrendered completely.

"Oh God, you're so hot." Hope inched closer. She trailed her finger from his imprisoned wrist to his shoulder, detouring on the way to test the firmness of his biceps. Being petted had never gotten him so horny before. His cock jerked, rising to tuck closer to Wyatt's body.

"You *are* awfully ready, aren't you?" Wyatt's eyes darkened, embodying that intoxicating storminess Clay adored. "Hope, take his bottoms off."

Whether because Wy didn't dare release his ultra-willing victim or because his fingers still hadn't recovered full motor skill, Clay wasn't about to object.

The feel of their girl's hand slipping between him and Wy—as he'd dreamed of for a week, no, longer—only fired Clay up more. He wished she'd move just a little toward his center. No such luck. No one was letting him off easy today. She eased the waistband over his cock, which felt ten times more swollen than usual. Heavy and hot, the bulk of it on his abs had him smiling. He could give as good as he got if Wyatt was in the mood.

The rare times his lover bent over for him were special. Wy wouldn't let anyone else have that much power. Except maybe one sassy cowgirl.

Clay lifted his ass a fraction of an inch to allow Hope room to work the material down his thighs then off his legs entirely. She combed the light hair dusting his shins and quads before boldly reaching between his legs to fondle his balls.

"Jesus, you two are going to kill me." He thrashed, or tried to, but Wyatt kept him immobile. The bigger man indulged their guest, allowing her to test the heft of Clay's nuts and coax them into drawing tighter to his core.

"More like drain you dry, but I promise you'll love being milked by us." Wyatt leaned in and gnawed on Clay's neck, just below his ear, in the spot that made his insides quiver like jelly.

The implication that he'd let Hope play along a bit had Clayton chomping at the bit. What a treat she made. Delicious. Sweet. Pure temptation.

Her pink-painted nail tapped Wyatt on the shoulder. "Kiss him. I loved watching you two make out the other night. It was like you were wrestling with your mouths. Talking without words. Show me again. More."

She didn't have to ask twice.

Wyatt held himself in an eternal push-up to avoid crushing Clayton. If his hand was still sore, he didn't give any indication. The strength he took for granted impressed Clay all over again. It always did. He wished he could run his hands along the length of the powerful form hovering over him. But he gladly settled for the taste of his partner's lips and the pressure of that sinfully seductive mouth bruising his in its urgency.

He'd always believed this was where Wyatt was most honest. Though the guy never uttered the phrase Clay would have liked to hear, he had no doubt about Wy's commitment and passion when the other man devoured him like this. How could he?

Together they succumbed, whirling around each other like straw in a dust storm.

Hope didn't let their intensity scare her. Instead, she nudged Wyatt's pants down his hips, then tapped his knee until he accommodated the removal of his clothes.

Their lightly perspiring skin conducted the electricity they generated when they collided like this. Raw power illuminated every corner of Clayton's soul. Wyatt's growl rolled over them like a clap of thunder when he settled himself between Clay's legs.

Wy's hips began the subconscious rocking that drove Clayton insane, particularly when the other man had already penetrated the tight rings of Clay's ass and filled him impossibly full.

Before they could make it to that irresistible stage of their lovemaking, Hope helped prolong the exchange. Or maybe exactly the opposite.

She insinuated her fine-boned hand between their damp abdomens. Seeking. Finding. Her fingers closed around Clay's shaft, inspiring a groan. He fed the desperate sound to Wyatt, pleading wordlessly for relief. Of whatever variety they chose to impart.

Only neither of the cowboys had the driver's seat.

An innocent young woman rendered them both incapable of denying her when she increased the ring of her thumb and palm to include Wyatt's steely length in her grip. *Damn*! With the two shafts combined into one overflowing fistful of wild Wyoming male, Hope began to work their erections in unison.

The gentleness of her supple palm contrasted with the hardness of Wyatt's cock and the stare the slightly older man drilled him with. Her infusion into their intense yet seductive mix had Clay ready to burst in a hurry. Not a record he would like to hold.

"Don't you dare." Wyatt nibbled on Clay's lip, not helping the situation in the least.

"What?" He played dumb.

"You think I can't feel how defined your head is where it's rubbing me? How much your cock is leaking as she spreads the wetness over us?" Wy's curt laugh held no malice. In fact, he seemed to tense at the idea of Clayton's desperation.

"You like it," Hope murmured, soft enough to slice through the guys' roughening arousal.

"Hell fucking yes, I do." Wyatt crushed his mouth over hers and let her taste the longing he had to have harbored in the moment. "More because you're touching me. Jerking me. Us."

Clay seized, all of him tightening in response to the gruff man above him and the tender woman bonding them. She patted Wyatt's flank as he propelled his dick through the tunnel of her hand, rubbing his erection along the full evidence of Clayton's similar hunger.

"Wy, I need you in me. Don't make me come like this. Empty." Clay hated that he cracked. But another orgasm—even if by her hand rather than his own—without that reassurance of their link might destroy him.

"It's been too long. You need a toy first. Something less..."

"Bulky," Hope supplied when Wy stalled, distracted by the squeeze of her fingers.

"Not going to last." Clayton gritted his teeth to keep from painting his come across the two observers right then and there. "Ride me. Please."

"He's cute when he begs." Unexpected shades of dominance highlighted Hope's allure. Damn, she really was a Compton after all.

Clayton reared up far enough to sink his teeth into Wyatt's shoulder, then uttered, "Now. Right now."

He regretted that his roommate would have to abandon their nest to grab the lube from their nightstand. Until Hope surprised him by dropping flat on her stomach on the mattress.

"What?" He didn't have long to wonder at her intentions.

She lunged forward, focusing on Wyatt's cock and angling the fully erect flesh toward her parted lips.

Both Clayton and Wyatt stared as she lowered her head and proceeded to demonstrate her proficiency at the lessons they'd taught her by laving Wyatt with sloppy kisses and licks that left him saturated. Slick. Good enough.

Rough and raw, this fuck would check all Clayton's boxes for a hell of a fun time.

If it hurt some, he'd only enjoy it more.

Wy knew. He didn't object. Muscles in his jaw ticked as Hope treated him to torturous slurps that left him thoroughly soaked. After far too long and yet not nearly enough pleasure, Hope lifted her head and smiled at Clayton.

"Thanks." He grunted when Wyatt wasted no time aligning the fat head of his cock with the puckered entrance to Clay's ass.

"Looking out for you." She winked. "Now show me how much you like it when he makes love to you. At least I'll know what I'm missing out on."

Clay whimpered. Not from the pain caused by the constantly increasing pressure the blunt cap of Wy's dick administered. But because of the flicker of rejection he caught in Hope's stare. Slighted, insecure and devastated, she mirrored his own painful cocktail of emotions. At least the ones he'd sometimes endured when she wasn't there to guide Wyatt, tease him into complying with her wishes and his own desires.

Clayton flung out his hand, latching onto hers and holding her tight.

A warm smile crossed her bee-stung lips. "You can take him. He's opening you. You're yielding. That's so hot."

As if her commentary drove Wy as nuts as it did Clayton, the bigger man breached his resistance. The first thrust of Wyatt's cock as it drilled into Clay's body stole his ability to correct her misconception. His grip had more to do with her tugging his heartstrings than Wy plowing his ass, though that was pretty spectacular too. Pleasure and a healthy heaping of pain twined into the perfect sensation as impulses ran up his spine, straight to his brain.

Endorphins more powerful than the drugs he'd tried as a teen rushed through his system. No matter how much he'd attempted to love that chemical high, which had enthralled his mother, it'd never held a candle to the rush inspired by sex with Wyatt. He'd grown out of that phase fast. Or should he say he'd been screwed out of it. Wyatt had saved his life, kept him from crashing down the same path as his mother.

Before the stale memories could cloud his relief and enjoyment, Hope returned him to the perfect present. She trailed her fingers along the rigid flesh twitching on his abdomen. Eventually she traced Wyatt's circumference, thrilling both men simultaneously.

When Wy began to pick up steam—his rhythm sure and as familiar as if they'd done this just yesterday—Hope took advantage of the slight gap between the men's torsos, necessitated by the upright position Wyatt drew himself into as he dug deeper, fucked harder.

She nestled Clayton's erection in her cupped hand, matching the shuttling of her fist with the hammering of Wy's hips. She kept time well enough that Clay imagined what it might be like to bury himself in her over and over while his roommate pleasured them all from behind.

"Oh, shit." He gritted his teeth and squeezed his eyes shut against the enticement of his vision. Still, he didn't act fast enough. Their joint efforts triggered the initial stages of his orgasm.

"That's right. Show her how hard you're going to come for us." Wyatt's flushed cheeks and the droplets of sweat trickling down his chest proved he would join Clayton. Considering how recently he'd been ill, the quick session could have been a blessing in disguise. Maybe Hope would believe him if he professed to have shot faster than a rookie's ride on a bucking bronco out of concern for his partner.

Not likely.

She surprised and delighted him again when she leaned in close and flicked the tip of her tongue over his tight nipple. The bite of her small teeth, which teased the nub, sealed his fate. He threw his head back, burrowing into the feather pillow. Wyatt scooped his legs up, supporting the backs of his knees with those big, healing hands.

The position opened him, allowing Wy deeper inside. Right where Clayton wanted the man. At the same time, Hope redoubled her efforts. Her fingers flew over his straining cock, the sides of her hand knocking into the ridge made by his engorged head.

She lifted her mouth from his chest to smile at him.

That simple lending of encouragement tipped him into rapture. Pulses rippled through the base of his cock. His balls gathered, then pumped his release from their depths.

Hope kissed first the raised tendons in his neck then his mouth lightly before the first stream of scalding come jetted onto his chest. Wyatt couldn't resist the stranglehold Clay's ass had on his embedded cock. By the time the third slash of pearlescent fluid left a trail across Clay's body, the bigger man joined him. Liquid heat flooded Clayton, rejuvenating his pleasure.

Through it all, Hope continued to stroke him, drawing out every last drop of semen he had to spend.

When Clay supposed he'd never experience something as satisfying in all his life, Wyatt surprised him. The man he adored reached down and massaged the puddles of slickness into his taut muscles. He dropped lower when his fading orgasm stole his stamina. The glistening surface of Clay's chest seemed to make a satisfactory pillow.

Wyatt relaxed for an atypical second. He let his head loll in the crook of Clayton's neck while Hope petted them both, smoothing back their sweat-dampened locks. The gentle caresses impacted Wy more than his impassive eyes and slack muscles would lead an outside observer to believe.

"You're still hard," Clay whispered to his best friend.

"So?" Wy acted like the inhuman feat was no big deal.

"You haven't gotten your fill yet." Hope traced his spine to his tight ass, then slapped him. "What are you waiting for?"

Wy shook his head. "Clay's had enough. He's going to be sore tomorrow."

As much as he'd like to disagree, Clayton detected a low-level burning he didn't dare aggravate with another round. "I'm sorry."

"Don't be a dumbass." Wyatt retreated gently, slipping from Clayton's body and leaving him bereft. "You have nothing to apologize for. That was—"

Hope cleared her throat. "It was fucking sexy and so damn beautiful. Now it's my turn."

"What?" Wyatt waved her off with a slice through the air. "No way. Your first time shouldn't be like this. Not with us either. You've saved yourself this long. Wait for the right guy."

"You *are* the right man. Men." Hope didn't blink as she uttered the truth.

"No." He refused to listen. "That guy would treat you to flowers and candlelight. Romance. Forever. The best I can do is a rough fuck."

He glanced at the wreckage they'd left on Clay's chest.

"I didn't hear any complaints." Hope chuckled, monitoring Clay's recovery.

"No, but Clay can take care of himself with the ranch hands. What will you do when they corner you and ask if the rumors are true? Someone always finds out around here. Some idiot will blab what they know. And you'll be facing unwanted attention every time you wander across some creep's path."

"You think my dads would keep those kinds of guys on the ranch?" She dismissed his concerns. "Quit making excuses, Wyatt."

Hope's eyes began to mist over and Clayton wanted nothing more than to hold her, rock her and take some of that pain away. Instead of coddling her, Wyatt grew harsh. He went for the throat. "What makes you think I want you anyway?"

"I may be a virgin, but I'm not a moron." She stared at the guy's stiff cock.

Clayton felt his dick stirring as they argued.

"Go ahead. Sit there and watch. Tell me you don't want me." Hope surprised him when she shoved Wyatt toward the mound of pillows against the headboard. He arranged them to provide himself the best vantage for viewing her display.

"If you weren't such a chicken, you could have had me already." This time she included Clayton in the beam of her laser glare.

He cleared his throat. "If that's what you really want, Hope. I'll give you anything you ask for."

"You will not." Wyatt whipped his gaze to Clay.

"You're not my boss." He huffed. "Well, shit, you kind of are. But not here. Not today. Never like this."

"No." Hope crossed her arms over her chest. "I'm not putting you in the middle of this bullshit. I don't need two guys. Or even one. Hell, I've handled myself just fine until now."

She melted his ability to object or even to swallow to keep from choking on his tongue when she collapsed onto her back, propped up by her elbows. From this angle, the guys had a clear view of her assets.

Hope shoved the soft T-shirt she'd borrowed from Clay over her breasts. The modest yet firm mounds of her chest had him ready to howl. Wy too, from the pinched set of his mouth. Especially when she cupped them in her pretty, pink-tipped fingers.

Wyatt reached out to help, but she wouldn't have it. Hope smacked his wrist, careful even in her ire—and through the haze of her arousal—to avoid his injuries.

"Get your hands off me. How do you like it? Being able to watch but not touch?" She rubbed the ache in her breasts, down her stomach to her mound. "I can be selfish too. Neither of you can have me. I'll take care of myself."

Wyatt shook his head like a dog emerging from a pond and encroached on Hope's territory. She put one foot on Wy's shoulder and shoved until he tumbled backward, taking up the spot next to Clayton.

"If you touch her, she'll stop." Clay's vehemence had Hope's pupils dilating. Made her wetter. Her fingers glided faster. "At least let me have this much."

"Fuck." Wyatt collapsed, drawing Clayton to his heaving chest. "Fine. Torture yourself. See if I care."

"Close your eyes if you don't want to see," Clay snapped at Wy.

"Sure." He groaned. "You'd have to superglue them shut to keep me from peeking."

Hope's self-caresses grew bolder. She demonstrated how she liked to be touched, rougher than Clay would have guessed. Then again, nothing about her had turned out to be like the spoiled, clueless princess of Compton Pass they'd unfortunately assumed her to be at first.

Her front tooth threatened to open the cut in her pouty bottom lip.

"Careful," Wyatt rumbled a warning.

Which she ignored.

She spread her legs wider. Wyatt lifted his head from the pillow to sniff the air. The scent of strawberries and Hope's cream perfumed their modest bedroom. Delicious. Ripe. Clay wanted to devour her like a juicy piece of fruit.

He knew she'd taste delicious too.

The fidget he gave as he sidled in her direction was shot down by a raised brow and the pause of her hands on her lovely rose-hued skin.

"Okay. Staying put." He kicked himself over and over for allowing Wyatt to dictate his lack of involvement. If he ever got another chance with her, he'd take it. Wyatt be damned. The man didn't understand that sometimes people simply needed. Even if the poison they craved wasn't healthy. Sometimes it didn't matter.

Their instant chemistry crackled in the space between them.

Hope began to run her fingers in spirals around her clit. The shaky gasps and whimpers that left her throat made Clay feel a tiny bit better about his seeming lack of control while Wy had tunneled into his ass.

What she did to him. And to Wyatt.

Oh Jesus.

Trembles wracked her slight frame and the rickety bed they shared along with it.

“Gorgeous,” Wyatt whispered. Clay wondered if the other man realized how hard he was hugging his partner. How tightly he clutched Clayton in order to avoid launching himself at the beauty they’d tamed and roped into bed with them.

Yet somehow hadn’t taken.

Clay tried to engage his brain but most of his blood still pooled in his crotch.

“I loved watching you,” she told them in between pants as she mimicked the pattern of penetration Wy had used on Clayton with her fingers, which tapped against her pussy. Occasionally they delved in as far as the flexible barrier that had kept her out of his clutches would allow.

Soon moans and curses, those dirty little swears, floated from the succulent mouth now parted as if permanently. He could easily slip his dick between her teeth. And no matter how she spit at them, he knew she’d welcome a taste.

Hope’s fingers flashed. They rubbed and nudged and danced where the contact did the most good. Fluttering everywhere, she quickly brought herself to the cusp. It was easy to tell she toed the line when her cheeks blossomed with a flush and her lids began to sink.

“Go ahead,” Clayton encouraged her. “Let yourself feel how right we are together. Even if we’re not touching. It doesn’t matter.”

She nodded and focused.

Within seconds the pitch of her whimpers and moans escalated.

“Now, Hope. Come for us.” Wyatt pulled the trigger and Hope shot off like a rocket on the fourth of July.

Both men stared, dazzled by the spectacle.

When the explosive relief of Hope's orgasm wore off, she couldn't believe what she'd done. The pair of sexy cowboys drove her insane with need. The bitterness that crept into the void left by her receding ecstasy made her sick despite the awe etched into their handsome faces.

They'd reduced her to retaliation.

That wasn't what she'd had in mind at all. *Shit.*

"The pair of you make me feel like I need to chomp down a fucking handful of oxcarbazepine."

They stared at her long and hard enough their eyes must have dried out. A proverbial cricket chirped in her mind. "It's what you use to treat bipolar disorder. Up down, up down. You hold out your arms, then shove me away. Enough. Fuck you and fuck you too. *Almost* everything isn't going to cut it."

"That's exactly what I've been trying to tell you, Hope." Wyatt dared to open his mouth. "We can't be what you need long-term. It's fun to play, but I didn't want to hurt you. That's the only place this can go unless you're willing to keep it entirely physical..."

"Clayton might have hung around for decades, accepting your backhanded rejection, loving you even when you shut him down. I'm not that strong. Sorry, Clay, I changed my mind. I'm going home."

She clutched the bunched shirt and shimmied it lower.

"Like that?" He reached for her. Though bare enough in the T-shirt to be some people's definition of indecent, she ran. "Hope, wait—"

"Put some damn pants on!" Wyatt roared at her.

She flashed him a one-fingered salute as she marched out of the house and away from them. The bonfire they'd roasted her blossoming dreams on kept her plenty warm in the spring night air.

When she got to her house, the lights were on and her cousins were waiting. They bundled her in their arms and her favorite blanket while Daniel notified Wyatt and Clay of her safe, if devastated, arrival.

Damn them for caring a little yet not enough to risk it all.

Chapter Ten

"I wonder what Vivi wants," Hope's mom, Lucy, speculated. She and Hope's dads had swung by the Compass Girls' bungalow on the way to the main house to pick her up.

Rather than add to her dishonesty, Hope simply stared out the window and tried not to seem too worried. Maybe she could breathe again with this secret off her chest. Unfortunately, the easing of her burden would come at the expense of her parents' grief.

At least she and her female cousins had already processed the horrific news. They could help the older generation cope. Or at least that was the plan. They'd gathered all the literature they could to help both the Compass Brothers and their families understand the prognosis, the trials already attempted and the inevitable decline that had accelerated recently.

I wish Wyatt and Clay were with me. Wy would let Clay do all the talking, and touching. He'd guard them, stoic, and have their backs while they cried enough for him too. She cursed under her breath when she realized just how much she'd come to rely on their support and protection in such a short period. Foolish. She didn't need anyone but her family. Tonight they'd stand together.

That didn't mean she didn't crave a little bit more. Selfish yet true.

"Doug thinks Vivi might be getting us a pool. If construction starts now, we figure it could be done by summer vacation." Austin bounced in his seat.

"She's not putting in a pool." Best to nip that idea right now, Hope figured.

"What makes you so sure?" Her mom rotated from the bench seat—where she perched between their two dads—her laser focus scary as hell. "She worships her grandkids and these four boys have been hounding her practically since they could talk. I wouldn't put it past her."

"It's a ridiculous idea." Hope rolled her eyes and even flipped her hair over her shoulder, shielding her heated face from her mother's scrutiny.

"Is not." Austin crossed his arms over his chest. She regretted the sting of her rejection. The Compass Girls' little brothers were always trying to impress them and prove they were plenty grown up enough to hang with their big sisters. In Hope's case, that went double.

Almost ten years separated her and Austin. Her mom always said she'd gotten lucky getting pregnant once. Twice had been a brilliant surprise. And so Hope had a little brother who idolized her. She did her best to live up to his admiration.

Hope swallowed hard. Protecting him would be impossible tonight except for crushing his expectations early on. The Compass Boys adored their grandmother right back. The next few hours would change them all forever. And this time she wouldn't even have Clay's warm arms around her as she recovered from the stabbing pain in her chest or the distraction of Wyatt ravaging the other man to yank her from her mourning.

Wy had warned her. Still, it stole her breath to be alone after a taste of more.

They didn't have to be lovers to stand by her. Well, maybe the effort wasn't worth it to them if they didn't get to screw her. No, *wouldn't*. Damn them.

Shaking her head, she focused on the hurdles ahead.

Her dad pulled onto the main ranch road. Lights streamed from the house and vehicles littered the yard. Strings of LED bulbs fashioned to look like half-melted candles in antique mason jars ringed the parking area and illuminated the stairs like a runway leading to crash site rather than a flight to paradise.

Hope floated from the backseat of the extended cab thanks to the unflinching grip of her dad's arm. She paused to hug him when he set her down gently.

"Thanks, kid." He ruffled her hair, then skimmed his thumb over the last vestiges of her black eye. A muscle in his jaw ticked. "Don't know what that was for, but I'll take it. Thought maybe you'd grown out of those by now."

"Just wanted you to know how much I love you." Horrified, she sniffled. Vivi was her dad's mom. He would need plenty more where that came from before the night died. But if she didn't act fast she'd blow the secret she and her cousins had slaved to keep for the past year. It was their grandmother's right to share the news.

Someone called her name just then. Unsure whether to curse or cheer, she spun toward the figure jogging from the direction of the barn. Mussed hair, a trim waist and the triangular shadow around his neck would have pinpointed the man's identity even if she didn't recognize the sound of his voice. The one that had cried out with pleasure as his partner showed her exactly what she was missing.

"Hope!" Clay's shout seemed nearer the second time. His racehorse legs ate up the distance between them. Wyatt followed at a more sedate pace, as if unconvinced by his bunkmate's enthusiasm.

Damn it, exactly nothing had changed.

Yet she couldn't help but smile, glad to see the pair, if even for a few seconds, before this difficult discussion. They'd help her steel herself.

"Don't take too long." Dad tugged one of the long locks of her hair. "Looks like we might be the last here. I want to hear more about this pool project of Vivi's. So don't make me wait."

Austin cheered as he raced into the house with their daddy and mom.

"I won't. Promise." She swallowed as her heart constricted.

Her hardass father surprised her when he bent low and whispered in her ear, "Those two dumb shits have been in a pisser of a mood since the weekend. They miss you, baby. Whatever they did, maybe you should go easy on them for it. Just this once."

"Whose side are you on?" She glanced over her shoulder wide-eyed at her dad. He'd never encouraged her with John. His opinion meant the world to her. Too bad the guys didn't actually want her like her dad thought.

"Always yours, Hope. I think they might be good for you. Tough enough to handle a Compton." He tapped the relic of a watch he always wore, the one that had been his father JD's. It didn't even have a digital display, never mind GPS or any of the more modern features standard on today's devices. He raised his voice to address the guys as well, "Five minutes. No more. Come on inside with her if you haven't finished your business by then."

"Thank you, Silas." Clayton had obviously caught the tail end of her father's invitation.

"Don't fuck up when it comes to my daughter or I'll make you *wish* you were mucking stalls for the rest of your life." The icy glare he leveled at the cowboy would have had poor John screaming as he peeled out.

Not Clay, or Wyatt, who stood behind him.

"Yes, sir. Understood." Clayton's respect warmed Hope's heart.

Once her father had been swallowed by his childhood home, Wyatt broke the silence. "Is she going to come clean?"

The dark centers of his eyes reflected the bright points of the electronic candles and the fireflies beginning to swarm around them.

"Yes." A small sob escaped though she attempted to clamp down on the noise.

"I won't say it's going to be all right." Clayton didn't hesitate. He bundled her into his arms. Though they'd never be lovers, he offered her solace and she gladly accepted. "We all know that's not true. But you'll get through it. You're a fighter."

"Your family is united." Wyatt reassured her. She thought she might have felt the brush of his knuckles over her hair but she couldn't be sure. "Together you'll make the best of things. You'll survive."

"Is that really enough?" She twisted in Clay's arms. "I'm sure Vivi wouldn't settle for less than thriving. She didn't when she chose JD over her original suitor."

"Look at you using those funny words. You must enjoy the notes you're taking from her." Clay hugged her, erasing the snark in his good-humored jab.

"I am." She bit the inside of her lip. "And I should go. Be with them. Keep this from dragging out anymore."

"Don't worry. Your Vivi's in the barn still. I saw her sitting in there with the old-timer, Jake. We left to give them some privacy since she looked so serious. Anyway, I saw you and...I just wanted to say sorry." Clayton cupped her shoulders and turned her to face him once more. "I hate how things ended up the other day. Wyatt's been telling me to leave you alone. I don't think I can anymore. I wondered what you've been doing, how you were. I've missed you, Hope. So much."

"Same goes." She swallowed around the lump in her throat. Though she glanced over at Wyatt, his inscrutable stare gave her no comfort. "I'm not sure that's enough, though."

Wyatt blinked. His lips parted. But whatever he was about to say didn't escape before Vivi and Jake interrupted. The veteran ranch hand had been a fixture at Compass Ranch since the golden days. He'd worked for JD while her dad and uncles had been away, exploring the world outside their tiny town.

The man held a special place in the family's heart for reasons she didn't think she fully understood. Something about the way he treated her Aunt Cindi had Hope on high alert. The Mothers always dismissed her curiosity on the subject, though. An eternal bachelor, Jake sometimes radiated loneliness that put fear in Hope's soul. She didn't want to end up like the kind man. What was his story, she wondered?

Maybe she'd ask Vivi when her grandmother was having a particularly lucid day.

"Hope." The elation she felt at the older woman's recognition faded fast. "Come inside with Colby and Silas. I need to talk to you."

Rather than argue with the slightly confused woman, Jake waved toward the house. His motion, hidden behind Vivi's back, commanded the two younger hands to comply with her directive.

When they reached the top of the stairs, Hope's grandmother put out her hand, palm perpendicular to the ground, commanding them to stop. "Sorry. I got confused for a second. Anxiety seems to exacerbate the problem."

The guys rushed to convince her it didn't matter.

"Shush. This is important." Vivi strained, leaning against the arm Jake wrapped around her tiny waist. Was she shrinking? She beamed at her granddaughter. "Another story for you. A quick one. And a lesson for you boys. Wyatt. Clayton. Yes. My Hope's boys."

"Everyone's waiting, Vivi." Hope shivered at the urgency in her grandmother's tone.

"They'll hold. I'm the one with the ticking bomb in my brain. And this is what I want you to know. Sometimes history repeats itself. Occasionally we get a do-over and I'm looking at one right here. I kick myself for all the time I let your father waste when he holed up in Alaska. Do you know why Silas ran off?"

"To work on the oil rigs." This was nothing Hope hadn't heard already.

"Wrong." Vivi snickered. "He was hiding. In deep freeze. Because he was terrified he'd hurt your mom. Or Colby."

"Sounds familiar." Hope tipped her head. "Why the hell did he think that was a good idea?"

"That son of mine is gallant to a fault. Willing to sacrifice himself for the happiness of his loved ones. Except he discounted how important he was to that equation. They were content, your mom and daddy. But not whole. And even when your dad came home with his leg mangled, then fought his way back to health, trouble followed. Your mom used the chance to show him just how competent she was. Wouldn't matter if people talked about the three of them—tried to put her down or treat her bad because of her choices. She could handle herself damn well. Did you know she held off a crazy man in the foreman's cabin at gunpoint?"

"Seriously?" Wyatt's eyes had gone wide.

"My mom makes it seem less dramatic than all that." Hope shrugged.

"Because to her, it was nothing. Not compared to the trauma of living without part of her soul for a decade then almost losing your dad again once she thought she could count on him to stick. After the incident, he had faith in her. Knew that had he been there with her, the whole thing would have gone down differently. His fear left her exposed. We all got lucky that night, and it could have been avoided had he not bolted again."

Hope nodded. "I can take care of myself too."

"Of course you can, girly." Vivi chuckled. "You're one of my Compass Girls."

"Tell that to the guy who gave her the black eye," Wyatt grumbled.

"She's safer with you than without. Could an accident happen? Or an on-purpose by some sick bastard like her ex? I suppose. But don't assume the worst-case scenario, okay? You don't want to wander through this life alone, son." Vivi touched Wyatt's cheek softly. He didn't evade her maternal caress. Instead he leaned in. "Believe me. I've been at it a while now. Jake here too. It sucks."

The grizzled ranch hand kicked at the decking with the scuffed toe of his boot.

"The years with JD by my side were a pleasure, even when things went to shit. Through it all we had each other. Isolating yourself—in here or here—" She tapped first his temple then his chest. "Won't keep bad stuff from happening. No. It'll mean you deal with problems in solitude. Dooming your partners to the same fate, one they wouldn't choose, isn't honorable. It's shortsighted. And cowardly. Don't make the same error I've seen before. Please. Don't hurt my Hope like that."

Tears tracked silently down Hope's cheeks as her grandmother pled her case.

"Truth is, the people we love have boundless power to inflict pain and devastation on us. Like I'm about to do to every single member of my family. But it wouldn't hurt so much if it weren't the most important bonds we threatened."

"But I don't want to—"

"Cause them pain?" Vivi sighed and patted Wyatt's cheek. "What do you think you're doing now? Afraid someone else will do the job because of what you have together? Would you rather your soul mates stand alone, or with you by their side? Times are changing. Hell, equal marriage laws say the three of you could even give me another wedding to remember. For a bit. Wise up. Quit wasting time. You'll really regret that one day. Trust me. Every second is precious."

"Believe me, I know." A shadow crossed Wyatt's deep, warm eyes.

"Son, the universe doesn't always keep the people we love safe. No matter how beautiful a life is, it ends eventually. And yes, those left behind suffer. But they have amazing memories to carry them forward. What will you have if you let go now?"

"I—" He blinked.

"It's okay, Wy." Hope snuck around Clayton to include him in her hold. "We'll look out for each other, through the good and the bad. With three of us, our odds are better, aren't they?"

"Well, yeah, I guess."

Clayton trembled beside them. "I love you, Hope Compton. Progress. It's sinking in through that thick skull of his. I don't know how, but you and your Vivi are working miracles this week."

"It's just the truth. I'm willing to trust you guys with all of me. And I would shelter you in my heart forever in return.

Destroy the chance now. Or lose it naturally later. It's up to you, Wyatt."

She and Clayton held hands as they separated from their would-be lover.

They didn't make it more than a few inches away before he growled. "Don't go!"

"That's better." Before any of them could react to Vivi's bluntness, she leaned on Jake, who escorted her inside. "Get your asses in here. You can make up later. Careful not to slam the door!"

"Yes, ma'am." If Wyatt's usually gruff voice seemed raspier, no one called him on it. Especially not when he lunged forward, clasping one of Clayton's hands and one of Hope's. He led them inside, refusing to let go even when they stood in the center of a roiling den of Comptons—by blood or by affiliation. As part of the ranch, and through their association with Hope, they'd earned the designation too.

Vicki Compton cracked hundreds of hearts that night, including those belonging to people not in the room to hear her confession firsthand. All of Compton Pass was impacted as the wave of her misfortune spread like a plague from home to home through the town she'd help nurture. But together, the family she'd built and the people she'd touched joined forces to patch the damage. As one, they healed each other. They wove around one another to form a safety net that promised catch whoever stumbled on the long road ahead.

Vivi gave Hope, Wyatt and Clayton a watery smile when she spied their linked hands during her announcement. The three of them didn't untangle their fingers once during the millions of questions that followed. In fact, they held tight while people in the room cried enough tears to fill Austin and Doug's dream pool.

And when they said goodbye and left, they went together.

Chapter Eleven

"Why is the turn signal on?" Clayton's grip on Hope's fingers grew uncomfortably tight.

"Have you forgotten where Hope lives?" Wyatt didn't bother to address Clay's real question. Typical.

Anger simmered beneath her hurt. It must have boiled over Clayton's. "You moron. Didn't you learn anything tonight?"

"Other than how crippling it is to lose someone you love?" Wy snarled. "I already had a pretty good grasp of that concept."

"You know what? Let me out too." Clay might have flung the door open then tucked and rolled from the slow-moving vehicle if Hope hadn't maintained their death grip. "I'm done with this crazy ride."

"Sit your ass down," Wyatt barked, then kicked up a trail of dust as he angled the truck toward their nearby bunkhouse. "Jesus. Fine. We'll talk. All three of us. About where we're going."

"I'm not fucking around, Wy." Clayton's soft utterance would have made that clear in any respect. "I can't do this anymore. I can't keep...*hoping*...without having. I really thought you'd seen the light tonight. That you got it. What Vivi tried to tell you. Son of a bitch. How can you still not understand? If you don't now, you never will. I'm done. This rodeo is over."

He slapped his cowboy hat on his jeans, launching a miniature cloud into the tense atmosphere.

Hope held on despite his shaking palm.

"You good with just me?" Clayton swallowed hard as his gaze melted into hers.

"Hell yes." She didn't give a shit about safety laws right then. Hope unbuckled her belt and scrambled into his lap. "I'd be so proud to be with an amazing man like you. Never let his emotional insecurity convince you otherwise."

The heated crush of his mouth cut her off before she could keep reassuring him of his potent attractiveness, both sensual and spiritual. So instead she showed him how she felt about the prospect of belonging to him. Calling him her mate would be an honor.

They got so carried away, she didn't realize they'd made it to the guys' cabin until Wyatt yanked the passenger door open.

"Get your shit if you're leaving." Wyatt's crimson cheeks made it seem as if Clay's decision eviscerated him. Yet it was hard to believe that from someone willing to live hands off—or heart off—forever.

"Fine." Clay sighed deeply, setting her aside as he prepared to uproot himself.

"You really mean it." The bigger man tipped his head like a confused puppy.

"Hell yes." Clayton winced. "I don't like it. Actually, I hate it. But I ought to be with someone who can reciprocate. And Hope doesn't deserve to be abandoned. Not because you're too fucking scared to man up."

"So you're saying I'm going to lose you both anyway? No matter how hard I tried to protect you?" His teeth gritted as he battled a force as strong and unyielding as gravity. No use.

"Pretty much." Clay nodded as he shoved past Wyatt and began retreating. "And now you won't even be around to watch my back. But it's better than lying to myself all the time, making excuses for you and always wondering why I'm not good enough."

"Hang on, what?" Wyatt turned fierce. Hope adored him even more when he raged against that insanity.

"You heard me." The other man threw his chin up and might have taken an impulsive swing if Hope hadn't rushed out of the truck to hug him from behind.

Wy seized the opening.

"Clayton Fisher, I *love* you. The capital-L kind. Don't you know that?" Wyatt grabbed Clay's shoulders and shook a bit. "How could you not?"

"When have you ever told him?" Hope wished she could have spared Clay the pain of his bruised soul.

"I didn't think the words were necessary." The dumbass closed his eyes tightly and let his forehead drop against his partner's. "Okay, shit, that's not true. The rush I feel every time you say it made it kinda obvious. Scared shitless. I couldn't."

"It's all right. I know it's not easy for you to express what's bottled up inside." Clay hugged his lover loosely around the waist. "You feel so strongly."

"For you I'd do anything." Wyatt opened his eyes. "Because I love you. Love. You. Clay. Don't leave me. I've got nothing without you."

"Ahem." Hope cleared her throat with abandon. It was either that or bawl. "You have me. Both of you. Whether you want me or not. All of me."

What finer show of their cores was there then the journey they'd made together these past two weeks? No matter what they let her have of themselves, she was willing to give everything she had to feed the vibrancy developing between them.

"Not yet. But we will." Wyatt flashed her a wolfish grin. "Right, Clay?"

"About damn time." He groaned. "Wait. I have a plan. Been daydreaming about this for a while."

"I *love* it when you're prepared." A hard slap on Clay's ass set the other man in motion. "Quickly. Go."

Wyatt ambled to Hope in the meantime. He gathered her to his heaving chest. "Thank you."

"For what? I'm pretty sure I've been a pain in your ass since you stumbled across me at Two Lefts." She grimaced against his thick muscles.

"I would have lost him. It was coming. Sooner or later. It took you to open my eyes." Steamy hints transformed his sexy bass into something irresistible.

"So you care for me because I helped you out with your boyfriend?" She kept her tone level. Thank goodness. Hysterics didn't suit her. Still she felt like the vintage toy Vivi showed her once. The yoyo had trundled up and down on a frayed string.

Hope didn't know how many more circuits she had in her before she snapped.

"Shit, no." Wy cupped her chin and tipped it up until she couldn't deny the honest delivery of his apology. "More like Clay and I couldn't connect until we found you. You're our bridge. The missing link in our chain. Without you, it never would have held."

"Oh." She pressed her hands to the fluttering in her stomach.

"Yeah." He smiled, an uncommon and beautiful sight, as he descended. For once, the press of his lips came gently.

Unhurried. Leisurely and light, as if he'd finally admitted to himself that they had time on their side.

After a minute or ten, his fingers snaked into her hair and tugged her head back, exposing her throat to occasional nips and kisses before he migrated to her mouth once more. This time he led with his tongue, seeking and finding permission to enter—her mouth, her body, her heart.

"Hope," he rasped against her lips as he stared into her eyes. "I have to have you."

"Yes, please." Begging didn't bother her. If they left her a virgin after tonight, she'd go insane. Everything was flawless. Perfect because they were there with her. Or would be if Clayton ever returned.

Before they got naked right there in the area shared by the rest of the bunkhouses, Clay rushed outside. He hopped the railing on their porch with his arms full and a bundle slung over his shoulder as if it were nothing at all.

"What the hell—?" She giggled at the wild array of colors and items he hauled like a hobo.

"Is that the pool you and Daniel bought the Compass Boys with the curse can money?" Wyatt laughed when he caught sight of the inflatable recreation beneath a stack of blankets. "Isn't it kinda chilly for swimming? Thought you were saving that for the first hot day."

"For once, just go with it. Improvise." Clay shushed his best friend as he deposited his supplies in the bed of the truck. "Shut up and drive. To our spot by the pond."

"Whatever you say." Wyatt paused to devour his boyfriend's scowl, which quickly converted to a grin. Though he'd sounded flippant, Hope knew he was working hard on sharing his feelings and maybe just a bit of control. The naked vulnerability he embraced for the sake of his partners made her fall even more in love with the man.

"Come on." She tugged at their shirts when they seemed about to say screw it and drop to the dusty ground right there. "I want to see this special hideaway."

The men broke apart, breathing hard.

"I'd like to get lost there with you both." Clayton swung her into his arms and dashed for the open door of the truck. They bounced along the dirt trail in relative silence broken only by Clay whispering sweet things to her or Wyatt cursing their journey. His goal lingered somewhat closer than the pond.

When they crawled down the narrow, spidery tire tracks that hinted at a lane, Hope glanced over at Clay. "This is my daddy's favorite spot on the ranch too. He says it's his thinking place."

"Guess we finally know who left the heart carvings in the pine tree." Wyatt winked at them. "They looked like they'd been there a while."

"Maybe he doesn't have as much to worry about these days." Hope smiled in return.

"What're the odds he'd show up here tonight?" Clay suddenly seemed nervous, and his face hosted a green cast.

"No way. He's with my dad and mom. He wouldn't leave them after Vivi's news. Not even for a second." She had no doubt.

"Hope, you realize what we're doing, right?" Wyatt parked the truck then put his arm around her shoulders against the top of the seat.

"You'd better be getting ready to fuck me." She loved the instant dilation of his whiskey brown eyes.

"Again with that naughty mouth." He hugged her to him and whispered in her ear, "We're going to take you tonight. Make you ours. But it won't be fucking. It'll be making love. Fucking comes later. Maybe tomorrow. Once you're an expert."

"You tease." She slapped his thigh, then scrambled out the other side of the vehicle in the space Clayton had abandoned a moment earlier. She rushed to see what he was doing.

Wyatt swung himself into the bed of the pickup to join his best friend. He slapped the insta-burst inflate capsule and monitored the progress of the pool as it puffed up.

"I see you've caught on." Clay grinned at his partner.

"Can you blame me? My brain was fuzzy from making out. I've got your drift now, though." He tossed the massive armful of blankets and even two pillows into the makeshift bed. Overflowing with softness and warmth, it was an inviting bubble away from reality.

While Hope peeked over the edge of the truck, standing on her tiptoes, she watched Clayton set the mason jars he'd packed up for Vivi, planning to replace them in the storage shed during his next shift, around the perimeter of their space. Finally, Wyatt withdrew some mosquito netting from the chest built into the rear of the truck cab. He draped it from a branch above his head so it cascaded in a lovely fall on either side of the nest they'd made for her and themselves.

It was the most romantic thing she'd ever seen.

"It's not very fancy—" Clayton chewed the inside of his cheek as he glanced over at her.

"It's perfect. Help me up." Raising her arms, she waited for each of her guys to take hold of one and lift her into the alternate universe they'd created. Diffuse light, the canopy of freshly budding leaves overhead and the peaceful song of young frogs lulled her instantly.

Tears stung her eyes. These stemmed from elation rather than the profound sense of loss that had assaulted her only an hour ago. How quickly things could change. Or maybe both extremes always co-existed in life and she had to focus on the positive to make it through. She could do that.

"Guys, I have to say something to you." She swallowed hard, praying she didn't ruin everything, but they had to know now. They were the right ones. She knew. Had known, just like Vivi promised. Crazy or not, here went nothing...

"Hmm?" Wyatt leaned in, kissing the tip of her nose.

"I love you." She actually heard the rush of Wyatt's breath as it burst from his lungs.

He dropped to his knees at her feet as if someone had slashed his Achilles tendons. Clayton braced the more muscular man, looking like he could use someone to lean on himself, before he spoke.

"Thank God. Okay, I admit it. I might have lied the other day. You know about the little-l thing. I graduated to the capital-L kind of love almost instantly. The night you and I sat on the couch, when Wy was so sick, I couldn't believe you distracted me. Or the way you took care of me. Made me feel like things would be okay." Clay took her hand. "I knew right then I loved you and would forever. It sounds dumb, but I was sure."

He clutched his chest as if tying himself together.

"You never have to keep things from me." She stood on her tiptoes to skim a kiss over his lips. "It's painful for you to hide the way you feel. You're not Wyatt. Do what's best for you. And he'll do the same. I can handle both, you know?"

"Thank God," Wyatt muttered again.

Then the time for confessions had passed. He wrapped a thick arm around the back of her knees and tugged, dropping her into his waiting arms. Without a shriek, she tumbled into them, trusting him to catch her. Behind them, Clayton had already kicked off his boots, unbuckled his belt and quickly shucked his jeans. From the corner of her eye she watched him strip his shirt over his head then free his full erection from the confines of his boxer briefs.

"Damn," she hissed when the sight of his glorious figure did funny things to the dampening flesh between her legs. She couldn't wait to touch him, taste him.

"No kidding." Wyatt held her out to his very naked partner.

When Clay accepted her, rocking her against his bare chest, Wyatt followed suit. Or unsuit. She swore she heard seams rip as he divested himself of his clean yet well-used garments in a hurry.

He lowered himself into the squishy paradise they'd constructed for her, making them laugh when he wobbled and cursed. Though the bottom of the pool was thinner than the sides, the advanced polymer they used in them these days still had plenty of squish to cushion them. As soon as he'd settled, Clay transferred her to Wy's grasp once more before joining them in the impromptu bed.

Hope snuggled between the plush covers. Spring night air made her grateful for the toasty shelter and the heat radiating from the two robust men flanking her. A shiver that had nothing to do with the temperature ran along her spine when Wyatt attacked the button of her jeans while Clay inched the hem of her blouse up her abdomen.

"You're so damn pretty." Clayton worshiped her belly, then the bottom swells of her breasts. "Beautiful too. But, even better, *pretty.*"

He traced the floral print of her cotton bra. Simple pleasures had always been her favorite. She had a feeling she was about to add a new one, right at the top of the list.

Silky hair fanned between her fingers. When had she tangled her hand in his wild locks? The other searched for Wyatt. When she found him, it was *there.* Like a heat-seeking missile, she curled her hand around his fierce erection.

Wy groaned. He flexed his hips, feeding his cock through the circle of her fingers.

Velvet and hardness beneath, he impressed and awed her.

As Clayton kissed her, someone removed her jeans and the lacy panties she couldn't explain why she'd selected. Maybe because they made her feel a little powerful. The guys certainly seemed to appreciate the flimsy garment regardless.

Wyatt held them to Clay's face. He breathed deep and shivered on top of her, now nestling between her legs. They connected, skin on skin, and she cried out. Every nerve ending welcomed him home. She writhed, maximizing their contact.

Next, Wyatt walked her blouse up and over her head, tossing it into the grass beside the truck. He slipped his hands around her and unhooked her bra with a practiced flick that inspired a spark of jealousy in her core. That and a whole inferno of need.

Once he finished, he admired his handiwork. Completely naked, the three of them displayed themselves for the joy of their partners and drank in the sight of the two people who turned them on the most. Their sexy bodies were a feast for her senses.

Sleek muscles flexed before her eyes. The smell of clean men and even the slight flavor of salt arose on their skin. She touched—and looked and tasted—to her heart's content while they did the same to her. And each other.

Until the longing inside her grew. She cried out, needing more though she didn't know what. Her whole body tensed and released, restless against Clay's figure over her and Wyatt's beside her.

When she looked to Wyatt, a little panicked at the imperative demands of her body, he understood. "We're going to take care of you, sweetheart. Relax."

"Can't. Need you." She looked between them both, holding nothing in reserve.

"You're going to be her first, Clay." Wyatt cupped his lover's cock, stroking reverently along the impressive length, his knuckles skating across Hope's soaked slit. Still, they both knew he was more manageable than Wyatt's thick cock. "I'll be her last."

"But..." Clay froze. He swallowed hard. "I've never done this before. You know, taken someone's virginity. I want to make it good for her."

"You were the first guy I was with. The only one who's fucked me. You were as scared shitless as I was. And you were gentle. I'll never forget that night." Wyatt's smoky admission had both the guys' hard-ons perking up where they nudged her. "I seem to remember coming hard enough I thought I might have a stroke."

"Mmm." Clay rubbed himself against her like a cat. "I do sort of recall that myself."

Hope wished she could have seen it. "You'll have to reenact it for me later."

"Much later." Wyatt rubbed her pussy, drawing gentle circles through the wetness spilling from her, coating her engorged flesh. Then he tugged on Clay, leading him by the cock as if he were a recalcitrant horse.

He felt as if he were hung like one when the tip of his dick pressed ever so slightly into her softness.

She gasped.

Clay leaned down to kiss her with such sweetness, and so completely, that she relaxed. Allowing him to penetrate a tiny bit more. They went on like this, making out and fusing tighter as Wyatt supervised. He alternated his attention between suckling on her breast, taking tastes of her lips—or Clay's—and doing something suspicious with his hand behind Clayton's back, between his legs, that she couldn't see.

Soon, Clay tried to slide deeper but couldn't. He froze. "I'm there, Wy."

"Good." The other man took turns kissing each of them, staring deep into their eyes as he shared his soul and promised he was every bit as connected as they were.

"I don't want to do this alone." Clay's hand shot out. He gripped Wyatt's wrist and drew it between him and Hope. "You should be here with me."

"Can you take a little more?" Wy teased the edge of her cunt where it hugged the very tip of Clay's cock. Even joining that much with the other man awed her. She held him within her, tight and secure.

"Yes!" She appreciated their seclusion, which allowed her to shout and whimper and moan as she needed to vent the mounting pressure within her. Already the experience outstripped the orgasms they'd lavished on her in the barn. Or even the power exchange they'd allowed her to witness in their bedroom.

She'd never felt anything remotely this intense before. Awe dissolved any lingering nervousness.

Wyatt slid his finger alongside Clayton's cock, tracing the iron shaft to the spot where his blunt head tucked against the last evidence of Hope's innocence. A shock of discomfort had her sucking in a lungful of sweet spring air.

"That's right. Keep breathing, sweetheart." Clay leaned over to kiss her senseless. When she blinked up at him, the slight pain had long been forgotten.

"We're going to do this together." Wy glanced up to Clayton. The usually affable man had gone rigid, completely still, poised on the brink of pleasing her even as he inflicted a bit of pain. "It might hurt her some, but we'll be here to soothe her, comfort her and show her how worth it great sex is. Especially with someone, *someones*, you love."

"You really are learning." Hope reached for him, rubbing her fingers over his cheek. "I'm proud of you, Wyatt. Now, please, fuck me already."

"That mouth—" he bit her lip, then continued, "—is going to get you in trouble someday."

"I can't wait." Clay quivered between her legs as he watched her spar with Wyatt. They must have turned him on so much he could hardly contain his desire.

"Then don't." Hope felt Wyatt curl his finger, caressing Clay's cock inside of her.

The other man couldn't resist. He moaned, then proclaimed, "I love you Hope."

Wyatt advanced with him, plunging beyond her previous limits.

Sparkles danced in her eyes, competing with the stars above them. Dear God, he'd overflowed her, stretched her to the max. His cock spread unused tissue and surveyed the far reaches of her body in one long, slow stroke. Fully embedded, he paused.

Wyatt kissed away tears, which she hadn't realized she'd shed. They streaked over her cheeks.

Clay crooned to her, telling her how brave she was, how beautiful and how tight.

She snickered at the last one, causing a delightful shudder to echo through both her and Clay at the movement.

"Oh damn, don't laugh. You're going to make me come like an amateur." He panted when Wyatt reached between them, seeming to squeeze—hard—at the base of Clay's cock.

"Thanks." Her cuddly lover breathed a sigh of relief and blanketed her body, making their connection as complete as possible. "You fit me so well."

"I could say the same." She ran her hands over his shoulders and across his pecs, adoring the strength in his bunched muscles. Before she knew what possessed her, she'd grabbed his ass and spread his cheeks. "But I think you fit Wyatt too, don't you?"

"Technically, I think he fits me better..."

"Not tonight." Wy kissed Clay's shoulder to ease his rejection. "I'd like to come in her, too, if you don't mind."

"I understand." Clay panted. "But someday soon I want your cock in my ass as I fuck her senseless. I love being in the middle."

Hope moaned at the infinite possibilities. Could she do that too? Be sandwiched between them? Maybe not tonight, on her inaugural ride. But hell yeah, someday...

Before she could inform them of her plans, Wyatt surprised her, presenting his middle finger for her to suck. It felt amazing to draw on his body while Clay began to move, ever so slightly, inside her. Her eyes rolled back and she nearly choked.

Wyatt removed the digit, now slick with her saliva.

And suddenly, she knew what he intended. So did Clayton, if his shifting had anything to say about it. He spread his knees apart, and hers in the process, making room for Wyatt's hand at his rear while he subtly began to glide within her. Slowly, carefully, with all the tenderness she'd imagined he possessed.

He exceeded her expectations a thousand-fold, mixing raw need with his sweetness.

And when Wyatt used that wet finger to fill his partner, supply him with a poor—yet decent enough for the moment—substitute, Clayton took things to a whole new level.

He rutted against her, cherishing her body even as he used it for his own pleasure. Hope clung to his shoulders, thrilled to be able to bring him the same rapture he infused her with.

Wyatt seemed to snap. Suddenly he became chatty, rambling mischievous suggestions and oaths of epic proportions to them both. Each lusty phrase acted like a live wire on her system. Knowing she could do this to her men turned her on more. The spiral of need and fulfillment wound higher and higher until she found herself clutching Clay as if he were the only thing grounding her soul to the planet. Without the steady beat of his hips between hers and his shaft massaging her from the inside, she would surely have floated away.

Wyatt anchored them both with his similar treatment of Clay and his free hand roaming across every inch of her that he could reach.

"It's okay to let go," Wy promised her. "We've got you. You're not going anywhere but up. Again and again. We're nowhere near done with you."

The intensity of her reaction frightened her, but only for a second.

She stared into Clay's wide eyes and saw the same ecstasy mirrored there. Never had she dreamed it could be like this. Intimate in ways far more momentous than corporeal.

"Want him to flood your pussy, Hope?" Wy knew just how much that demonstration would enhance her desire. "His ass is tight on me, clamping down. Especially when I rub him right...here."

Clay cursed. His body shook. He went stiff as a board between her thighs. And still...nothing. He wrestled the reaction until he looked in her eyes. "Come with me. Please. Hope, please."

Nothing could have held her back then. The next time he ground forward, she instinctively arched her back, presenting her clit to the muscles at the base of his erection. They came together perfectly.

She exploded. The fullness of her pussy blew away every orgasm she'd had. Either by her own fingers or even Clayton's mouth last week. Nothing could compare to this.

And that was before the hot rush of his semen flooded her.

Once he began to shower her with the proof of his matching passion, she was lost. Spasms wracked her, causing her to wring jet after jet of come from Clay. The poor man seemed almost distressed as his pleasure lingered, making him dance as though electrocuted.

Wyatt didn't let either of them off the hook. He continued his steady assault on Clay's ass until the other man didn't have a single drop left to pour into her.

Several times, Hope tried to speak. To explain the euphoria coursing through her. But when Wyatt tapped Clay's hip and nudged the limp man aside, she realized her education wasn't yet complete.

"Hold on to it, sweetheart." Wyatt rubbed his cock against her still-throbbing pussy. The first contact rasped her over-stimulated nerves enough that she might have decked him if he were closer. "You can do it again. And again. If you don't let it fade."

She didn't quite believe him, but she was willing to try. Riding that rainbow over and over held so much appeal she feared she could get addicted faster than if it were some of the new mutations of crack or other super-drugs on the market.

"How sore are you?" Clay lifted his head from where it rested on her breast. "He's pretty damn big."

"It's okay." She'd feel them tomorrow for sure. But she didn't care. In fact, it pleased her to know their presence within her body wouldn't be forgotten easily. "Better than. Come on, Wyatt."

He didn't hesitate. Slippery from Clay's come, which overflowed her in decadent trickles, her pussy welcomed him as he burrowed inside her more easily than either of them expected. He had to work at it, but it didn't hurt. Instead, she realized he'd been right.

The embers of her lust flared to life, searing them both in the process.

She dug her nails into his ass and encouraged him to ride.

But he didn't.

Not at first. Instead he nuzzled their noses, simply reveling in the bonding of their bodies, hearts, minds and souls.

"I could come again just watching you two," Clay whispered. "You're perfect for each other."

"We all are." Wyatt kissed his mate before surrendering to the urges of their bodies. He pumped into Hope carefully at first, taking full advantage of the wetness left behind by Clay. "Damn, how long have you been saving that up?"

"Hey, I can't help it that you wouldn't do me. Just thinking about her gets me riled up. It's been a long week." He sighed, content. "Never again, right?"

"I couldn't give either of you up now." Wy increased the pace of his lovemaking. "This is where we belong. With each other."

Hope amused herself by rubbing her hands over every inch of the dominant man thrusting between her legs. She wrapped her arms around him, hugging him to her core. "I won't let go. Ever."

Clayton joined them, all of them exchanging a triple-decker kiss. The instant their tongues tangled, she lost it.

With a shuddering cry, she came, smothering Wyatt and dragging him into pleasure with her.

Clay reached between their legs. Probably to massage Wyatt's balls as he emptied them into her. The man fucked deep—tight—hardly leaving before pressing all the way forward again. He stayed buried inside her, fused as they both unraveled.

And still he was hard inside her.

"Again. You can do it again?" Her jaw fell open.

He looked beyond their constructed paradise and began to retreat. "Not tonight, you're not up for it. I don't want to h—"

"You can only injure me by pulling away. Remember?" Hope wound her arms around his neck and rolled as hard as she could to the side. Clayton instantly snuggled up to her back. Being cradled between the two men she adored salved any potential discomfort her untrained body experienced.

She had a lot of time to make up for. And so much to learn.

They were willing to teach her.

Finally.

Epilogue

Hours later, Hope reached for her phone. Wyatt grunted when she pressed into his ultra-relaxed belly with her elbow. Sometimes she forgot he wasn't as hard as he looked. "Sorry."

He flexed his abs, supporting her easily, and smiled. "You always catch me off guard. But I've got you, sweetheart."

With the device in her hand, she peeked at the incoming text before they could get distracted again. They'd spent half the night embroiled in lovely diversions already.

Where the hell did they take you? Are you okay? Do I need to rip someone's balls off?

Sterling. Oh boy. "If I don't answer this, my cousins are likely to scour the ranch until they find us and make sure you didn't break my heart again."

Clayton winced in the starlight. "I'll do my best never to hurt you."

"It's inevitable." She kissed Wyatt's wrinkled brow, then patted Clay's chest with her free hand. "Do you know how many fights there are on a given day between various members of my family? Hell, I've seen my parents' heads nearly explode before. And no holiday is complete without a couple of my uncles taking a swing at each other. But they always work things out. I'm not afraid of temporary problems. I believe in us. We'll be fine in the end, even when we disagree at first."

Clay lifted her knuckles to his lips and pressed a kiss to them. "With you I'm not afraid anymore. You'd better watch out, Wy. I'm about to get mouthy."

"I'm not sure I plan to complain about that. I like your mouth just fine." Wyatt growled softly and angled himself toward them. A little achy, Hope still felt her pulse picking up at the promise of more fun ahead.

Another buzz from the phone made her jump, putting a sliver of distance between them.

"Get under the quilt before you open the line." Wyatt bundled her between the firestorm created by his and Clayton's bodies. The blanket had been unnecessary for keeping warm. It made a nice shield for her nudity, though. Too bad if the rash from their five o'clock shadows or the purple circles of their claiming kisses shone through on her collarbones, shoulders and neck.

She grinned as she punched in the conference number, added her three cousins to the contact group then hit send.

"Where—?" Sterling answered immediately. "Oh."

"Ah, I see the situation is mostly under control." Jade shook her head as Sienna popped into the upper corner of the display. Nestled against Daniel's chest, she didn't seem likely to be moving anytime soon either.

"What the hell is wrong with this picture?" Sterling addressed Jade, her usual partner in crime. "The two good girls are getting some and we're sitting at home twiddling our damn thumbs with our little brothers and a ranch hand who's got no interest in Compton women."

Boone laughed from off-camera. "Hey, at least you don't have to worry about me pawing you. Unless you don't pass me that popcorn."

Sterling grumbled something about never getting laid again.

Daniel laughed, then patted the other side of his bed. "I'll make room. Come on over, ladies."

"You wish." Sienna must have pinched something tender beneath the covers as Daniel yelped and went a little purple. "Leave my cousins alone."

"Hey, Hope's got herself a pair. Why not go for three gorgeous women?" He shrugged, the adoration in his gaze as he peered down at his girlfriend making it clear he needed no one else to be happy.

"You couldn't handle a trio of Compass Girls." Jade snickered.

"Can't blame the man for trying," Wy joined in.

Hope's heart expanded in her already bursting chest. Not only had she found two perfect men to love, but they fit in perfectly with her family. Her cousins approved. A flash of premonition caught her off guard. She could see them all huddled around—laughing, talking, eating—at a million family gatherings to come. The guys shooting the shit, the Compass Girls plotting devious ways to hook up their baby brothers with women who'd mesh just as well into their ever-expanding clan.

Decades of joy and fun to offset life's challenges.

"I can't fucking wait," she whispered.

"For a fivesome with your cousins?" Clayton looked as eager as one of the herding dogs going for a car ride.

"Nice try, buddy." She laid a smacking kiss on his cheek. "You'll have to settle for me. For life. You're mine."

The smoldering possession in his gaze thrilled her and almost made her forget they had an audience.

"Ahem. Earth to disgustingly gooey couples," Sterling grumbled, then squinted. "You're about to lose your blanket

Hope. Bad enough your guys are flashing us all. And where the hell are you? Is that a truck? Are you outside? Isn't it too cold for that shit?"

"Plenty warm." Hope grinned as she shook her head. Wyatt and Clay reached for the corners of her quilt.

"Don't feel the need to cover up on my behalf." Jade scanned the guys, admiring their frames if her pausing gaze was any indication. "You know, the only thing that could make you hotter would be some ink. Hell, maybe we should get a tattoo, Compass Girls."

"Why not? Our dads all have them." Sterling nodded her agreement instantly.

"I don't know." Sienna nibbled her lower lip before peeking up at Daniel from where she rested against his chest. "What do you think of that?"

"Sounds sexy." He traced the curve of her shoulder. "But I think anything on you is hot."

"What would we get?" Jade seemed to be seriously considering the proposition. "Not the same back-piece as our dads have. It's gargantuan. It wouldn't fit on us."

"I think it should be something...girly." Hope smiled when Sterling wrinkled her nose. "Okay, not *too* froufrou, but different from those huge ones our dads have. Something for Vivi."

They all seemed to inhale simultaneously as they recalled the start to the evening. Hope would never forget the look on her dad's face when he'd found out. Or the betrayal on her mother's when she peeked over his shoulder at her daughter. Acceptance too. As a nurse, she had to have known something was up.

"But what?" Sienna asked, breaking Hope from her regret. She'd fix that first thing in the morning. Apologize. Her parents would understand. She prayed.

"You'll know it when you see it." Wyatt smiled down at Hope. "I think that's how these things work. Over-thinking it doesn't help. Just wait and when it's right—"

"It's like you just *know,*" Clayton finished for his partner.

"I know." Hope kissed first Wyatt, then Clayton.

"Me too." Wy deepened the exchange. "You two are mine. Always and forever."

Clayton and Hope didn't resist when Wyatt angled their faces toward each other then observed their lip lock. "And each other's."

Hope nodded, slowly separating from Clay, happy tears stinging her eyes where only sad ones had lingered before.

"Gross. Enough mushy shit." Austin bounced onto the couch beside Jade, covering his eyes as he peeked over the Compass Girl's shoulder. He must have opted to stay with his cousins, or maybe their mom and dads had needed time alone to cope. From the shouts in front of Sterling, there was some serious gaming going on.

"Learning curses from Doug, huh?" Wyatt raised a brow at the young cowboy. Hope couldn't believe he'd intimidated her with that look in the beginning. Now that she knew his secrets, his soft spots, he was in for a hell of a ride.

"Sorry, Wy." He sighed. "I mean, enough mushy crap."

This time Austin embellished the tame substitute by miming sticking his finger down his throat.

"I'm going to remind you of this conversation in a few years." Daniel shook his head. "You don't know what you're missing, kid."

"Nothing good. Not like ice cream. Or pools. Or my bike." Her brother tossed a dismissal over his shoulder before dive-bombing his cousins from the back of the sofa. Looks like Jade and Sterling had a full house, and their hands full too.

"Were we ever that hard to control?" Wyatt groaned.

"Probably." Clay considered for a second.

"You still are." She patted his chest. "But I'm up for the job. Not to mention maybe raising some of our own chaos."

The last came quietly, but Wyatt clearly heard. Beneath the covers, his hardness pressed into her hip, strong and eager to give her what she wanted.

Someday, now, whenever.

"I'd love to see you and Clayton blended into something so precious," he murmured.

"Okay, time to go." Jade might actually have sported a blush in the face of their intimacy. "Have a good night. Don't freeze your balls off."

"That's good advice." Daniel's brows knitted.

"I'll never be cold again," Wyatt said matter-of-factly.

"Me either," Clay agreed.

"Goodnight." Sterling sounded funny, as if she were crying again. "Compass Girls rule. Just remember I'm your favorite cousin. I want to be the maid of honor."

The three women chuckled as they disconnected, leaving the dark night sky and the two men Hope loved to illuminate the shadows. She winced. "Sorry. They don't know when to quit sometimes."

"You don't want to get married?" Wyatt spoke carefully enough to alarm her.

"Do you?" She looked between him and Clay. "And you?"

"Hell yes." They both roared at the same time.

"You're not getting away." Wyatt resumed his claiming by adding another mark to her neck. "Either of you."

"I'm not running." She fisted her hand in his hair, holding him close and seeking Clayton with the other. "Besides, my dads are likely to haul out their shotguns when they get a look at your handiwork here."

She gasped as Clay nipped below her ear.

"Well then, let's make it real obvious. Maybe we can elope tomorrow. I'm not exactly a patient man." Wyatt paused, growing serious once more. "I love you Hope Compton. And you, Clay."

"I love you too." They spoke together.

One voice.

One heart.

One future.

About the Author

Jayne Rylon and Mari Carr met at a writing conference in June 2009 and instantly became archenemies. Two authors couldn't be more opposite. Mari, when free of her librarian-by-day alter ego, enjoys a drink or two or...more. Jayne, allergic to alcohol, lost huge sections of her financial-analyst mind to an epic explosion resulting from Mari gloating about her hatred of math. To top it off, they both had works in progress with similar titles and their heroes shared a name. One of them would have to go.

The battle between them for dominance was a bloody, but short one, when they realized they'd be better off combining their forces for good (or smut). With the ink dry on the peace treaty, they emerged as good friends, who have a remarkable amount in common despite their differences, and their writing partnership has flourished. Except for the time Mari attempted to poison Jayne with a bottle of Patrón. Accident or retaliation? You decide.

Jayne and Mari can be found troublemaking on their Yahoo loop at:

http://groups.yahoo.com/group/Heat_Wave_Readers/

You can follow their book-loving insanity on Twitter or Facebook or send them a note at contact@jaynerylon.com or carmichm1@yahoo.com.

Sometimes life doesn't go according to plan.
Sometimes it's better.

Winter's Thaw

© 2013 Mari Carr & Jayne Rylon

Compass Girls, Book 1

Sienna Compton has it all figured out. Her life's goals are set and it is all systems go. At least, it was. Until her long-time boyfriend Josh threw a ringer into the master plan, requesting a "break" from their relationship. Now she's left alone during the long, cold Wyoming winter, questioning what her heart has always believed to be true love.

Daniel Lennon is facing an uncertain future. When a tragic accident leaves him unable to pursue his career as a professional bull rider, he finds himself at Compass Ranch, working to help Sienna's father, Seth, build his horse breeding business. One look at Sienna has Daniel envisioning things he never imagined wanting—a permanent home, love, marriage—and he's willing to use all the red-hot tricks in his sexual arsenal to melt the ice surrounding Sienna's broken heart.

When lust turns to genuine emotion, can Daniel convince Sienna to take a chance on something different and unexpected? Can he persuade her to consider a new path, one that will lead her directly to his arms…forever?

Warning: Roping and riding, past and future, cold winter and fiery desire, lust and love all come together in this new Compass series. Saddle up and hang on. The Comptons are back!

Available now in ebook and print from Samhain Publishing.

What do a madame and a bounty hunter have in common?
They want the same man.

River Bound

© 2011 Myla Jackson

Bound and Tied, Book 3

When Rosalyn Smythe, aka Madame Rosie, steps aboard the Marie-Dearie, she hopes it's the end of a year-long search for her runaway fiancé, Dalton Black. Her cabin holds a surprise: James McKendrick. Notorious bounty hunter, old lover…a man too happy to help clear the air—and her heart—of her murdering, thieving bastard fiancé once and for all.

In disguise as a riverboat gambler, Dalton is determined to find who framed him for killing two U.S. Army soldiers and who stole the gold they were carrying. He wants his life back—and his woman, who just happens to be on board and on the arm of his former best friend.

Convincing James he's innocent is easier than winning back Rosalyn's heart. Especially since Rosalyn seems to be enjoying their competition for her affections a little too much. There's only one place to work out his dilemma. In bed.

As the sheets become unbearably hot, threads of evidence leading to the real killer are unraveling, leading toward one fateful card game—and one man who's hell-bent on making sure Dalton has nothing left to lose.

Warning: This title contains hot ménage a trois scenes, bondage, and two men loving, sharing and fighting for the love of one woman with very specific bedroom desires and a bordello full of experience to tempt any man beyond redemption.

Available now in ebook from Samhain Publishing.

FANTASY - PARANORMAL - CONTEMPORARY - SCIENCE FICTION

SUSPENSE - LGBT - CYBERPUNK - STEAMPUNK - REGENCY - WESTERN - FANTASY - PARANORMAL - URBAN FANTASY

FANTASY - PARANORMAL - CONTEMPORARY - SCIENCE FICTION - HISTORICAL - WESTERN - ALTERNATE WORLDS

Any way you want it!

Print books and ebooks
available at
samhainpublishing.com

SAMHAIN®
PUBLISHING

It's all about the story...

SUSPENSE - LGBT - CYBERPUNK - STEAMPUNK - POST APOCALYPTIC

SAMHAIN®
PUBLISHING

It's all about the story...

Romance

HORROR

Retro
ROMANCE

www.samhainpublishing.com

CPSIA information can be obtained at www.ICGtesting.com
Printed in the USA
BVOW05s0349170615

404740BV00002B/2/P

9 781619 219540